Living, Loving, and Lying Awake at Night

Living, Loving, and Lying Awake at Night

by Sindiwe Magona

Interlink Books

An imprint of Interlink Publishing Group, Inc.
Northampton, Massachusetts

This edition first published in 2009 by

INTERLINK BOOKS
An imprint of Interlink Publishing Group, Inc.
46 Crosby Street, Northampton, Massachusetts 01060
www.interlinkbooks.com

Originally published in South Africa by David Philip Publishers (Pty) Ltd.

Library of Congress Cataloging-in-Publication Data
Magona, Sindiwe.
Living, loving, and lying awake at night / Sindiwe Magona.
p. cm — (Interlink World Fiction)
ISBN 978-1-56656-452-6 (pbk.)
I. Women—South Africa—Fction. I. Title. II. Series.
PR9369.3.M335L58 1994
823—dc20 94—4357
CIP

Printed and bound in the United States of America

To request our complete 40-page full-color catalog, please call us toll free at 1-800-238-LINK, visit our website at www.interlinkbooks.com, or write to Interlink Publishing, 46 Crosby Street, Northampton, MA 01060
e-mail: info@interlinkbooks.com

Contents

CONTENTS

For Fred
who gave me room to write

Glossary

amajoyini	migrant workers
amaXhosa	Xhosa people
arme	poor, poor thing
bakpot	literally baking pot, refers to heavy round iron pot, used for all cooking and bread-baking
bhuti	older brother, used as term of respect
blerry	bloody
doek	head scarf
donga	gully
en klaar	finished, or that's it
frikkadel	fish or meat balls
goed	good
hokkie	small shack
isishweshwe	skirt and apron made of brown or blue German print cloth
join	migrant labor system
koesisters	twinned doughnuts

GLOSSARY

kombi	minibus or van
krap	literally scratch, refers to nosing around
lekker	literally nice or nicely, means thoroughly, or really
lobola	bride price
mampara	fool, or one uninitiated in township ways
makoti	new wife
mlungu	white
mos platsak	literally flat sack or pocket, refers to being obviously broke
nogal	on top of everything else
oupa	grandpa or grandfather
plaasjapie	village yokel
pondok	tin or wooden shack
rondavels	round mud huts with thatched roof
shushu	Xhosa for hot or sunny
skelm	crook
skollies	anti-social renegades
slaps	left-overs or leavings
suurlemoen	lemon, refers to sour disposition
uhuru	liberation
umfino	wild leafy green vegetable, similar to spinach
vetkoek	fried dough
voetsek	be gone or away with you, used for a dog; when used to a person, considered very rude
wethu	hey you, to a friend or age mate

PART ONE

Women at work

1

Leaving

It was right at the time of night when dreams glue eyelids tight and spirits, good and evil, ride the air; when lovers stir, the fire spent once more rekindled; and the souls of the chosen sigh as they leave the flesh, homeward bound. A woman lay wide-eyed on her grass mat on the floor of a tiny, round, mud hut.

She was tired. Spent, body and mind. The tiredness of her mind and body and heart came together as one. It robbed her of sleep. It forced her to relive the day just past, the day she feared and knew she never wanted to see again. But fight against it as she did, the day kept painting itself in her mind's eye. Over and over and over, it kept pulling her back to itself and away from sleep and forgetfulness.

Eyelids sealed, she saw it all. Trapped. Unless?

As always, yesterday she had been up with the first bird's song. Long before morning broke, her day started. She had crept away from her mat; not to wake the baby still sleeping. Fear-filled, she went to the cardboard box where she kept food. Enough mealie-meal for today's morning porridge. If she made it really thin, used as little mealie-meal as possible, she could save some for the next day, perhaps. But maybe it would not be enough even so.

Getting up, she had not put the baby to the breast. That was drying up. Better to spread it over the day. Taking kindling, she went outside and started a fire. Wood from the faggot next to the hut was her fuel. By the time the children woke, the three-legged pot was boiling steadily away and the morning's nourishment was readying.

Soon the children, content, were happily at play or, those old enough, doing their little chores. The woman had fed the baby, put her on her back and then had gathered cow-dung from the nearby veld where the cattle grazed.

On her bared knees, skirt girded high, the basin of cow-dung next to her, she set to work. A scoop or two from the basin; thwax-thwax, onto the floor. Left hand steadying her, the right, like a knife spreads peanut butter on a slice of bread or a builder's spatula, cement on a brick, slowly and evenly, swept the dung across the floor: long whorls painted by her hand, painted wet green, the color of fresh cow-dung. One bit of floor at at time, until the whole floor was smeared; she spread her love through her fingers: dung and water and her tears mingling in her offering, seeping through her fingers as it spread sending its scent up her nostrils.

Then she went to the river. The pail swinging at her side sang its song of emptiness, the wind playing in its dry throat. Returning, it stood silent on her head; filled with life from the river, it was content and thus made no noise. Neither did the baby asleep on the woman's back. She had been fed and knew nothing of her mother's anxiety that her breasts were drying. The mother feared for her little one's life.

Two cups of mealie-meal, two breasts that were drying up, an old hen that had stopped laying eggs, an empty kraal from which she could no longer find even dry cow-dung to use in making a fire, so long had it held no cattle, and five children who daily needed feeding; these were the thoughts that traveled with the woman on her way to and from the river, and stayed with her the whole day through.

Now, as she lay awake, these same thoughts stole her sleep; stole her forgetfulness; robbed her of what little peace should have been hers in the middle of the night.

Gather berries from the forest. But autumn is a stingy season. Pluck *umfino*, wild spinach, from the veld if sheep and goats had overlooked any. Dig the same veld for roots. If you can beat the witchdoctor to it. She had spent the day thinking of ways out of her quandary. Now, in the middle of the night, the bothersome problem refused to surrender her to sleep and rest.

Weak, etiolated light flickered ineffectually at the far end of the room. On the naked floor that gleamed from the smearing of that day, stood an old small can that once, long ago, had contained jam or condensed milk or some other such. Through a hole in its lid a dirty kerosene-sodden rag sprouted. And it was from this contraption that a frail light made its valiant but vain attempt at splintering the dense dark of the room.

The woman, who wasn't quite thirty yet, slept in this little hut with her five children. She had been made a wife at a tender age, for that was the thing to do in those days, and each time her husband returned from the gold mines of Johannesburg, where he worked for eleven months a year, she was soon with child. Had all her pregnancies come to fruition, and had none of her babies died in infancy, there would have been perhaps more than double that number.

This moonless night her mind kept turning and turning, asking itself questions the owner had never heard asked of anyone before. Questions that both frightened her and left her feeling light as the down of a new-hatched chick.

If I leave, thought the woman, who will look after my children? Who will cook for them? And if one should be sick, what will happen? Before the answer came to her, other questions thrust themselves into her mind; burning it with their urgency: If I stay here with them, what shall we eat? If one of them should take sick, what shall I do? What is to become of us if I do not go?

Her husband was not one to remember his wife once he was in the gold mines of Johannesburg. As years went by the woman had come to realize this about him, and although she loved him still she had slowly come to accept that, unlike husbands of most women in the village, her husband would never be a provider: not to her, not to his children; he didn't even give his mother support. And that was, indeed, something, for in his own fashion he loved his mother greatly. Some would say inordinately so, in fact.

That night, the mind of the woman told her, "You only have a husband when his body can lie next to yours and his stick pushes up your thighs."

We have all these children, said the woman to herself, one for each time he has come back from the mines. But even that doesn't give my husband a heart. As soon as he leaves he forgets all about us.

In the barely lit room the mother could discern darker shapes on the floor, her sleeping children oblivious to the battle raging in her mind; in her heart. Somewhere in the middle of the room she heard a moan and knew it was Sizwe, the one after whom the baby came. How she could tell them apart, not just their faces but even their coughs, their laughs, and the way each turned himself or herself at night on their little grass mats. But then, she thought, if I couldn't do that, I would not be a mother.

If I couldn't do that; I would not be a mother. I would not, would not, be a mother; if I could not do that. That's it! screamed her brain, alerted to possibility. That's it. That is it. She said it as if she had stumbled on a gold nugget or a cool pool of sweet, clear water in the middle of a vast desert. A find. Salvation.

Her heart leapt. She had found the key: I will not be a mother that way. She would fulfil her obligations as she understood them and provide for them. The only way she could be a mother to her children, she saw, would be to leave them.

With the stealth of a cat about to mess, she moved. She did not want to waken any of them. With a pang, she thought of Nomakhwezi, her eldest, who slept like a hen; one eye open, foot ready to leap to wakefulness. Nomakhwezi was the most likely to awaken if her movements were but a little louder than those of a mouse.

She had got under her thin blanket fully clothed. Now, hand slid beneath the flannel petticoat she wore and reached up to her waist. There it was, confirmed her touch. Fingers rubbed; closing around the lump in the crude money-belt made from a strip from an old pinafore. There it was. She could. She rose and stood still and straight as a reed on her mat while her thoughts galloped away.

Pulling her blanket around her, she walked towards the door: slowly, carefully, and with heavy heart. She opened the door and stepped out.

Sheathed from head to ankle, face and feet met the chill of night as she softly closed the door behind her. For a brief moment she stood outside the door; stood still and listened to the breathing of her children. Her children, breathing in deepest sleep.

The woman listened and imagined she heard: mmhh-psshh, mmhh-ppssh; and could almost see the rise and fall of the baby's heaving form. Asleep. And trusting.

A thorn long embedded in her heart twisted itself: Ttssp!

A drop of blood squeezed out of her heart and lit the whole night-blackened sky. The stars showered light, making her path as bright as bright could be: Ttssp!

Clear as spring water beneath mountain boulders she saw her way: Ttssp. That was the spur. Ttssp ttssp ttssp.

Light as dandelion seed adrift in April's breeze she walked away from the hut where her children slept. Away she sped; swiftly, before the thorn-drawn drop of blood dried, giving her a chicken's fearful heart. Before she remembered that Thandiwe, the six-months'-old baby, would burst her lungs before cockcrow reaching for the breast that would not be there. That would come before the older children started the cry: *Uphi umama? Uphi umama? Umama uye phi?* (Where is mother? Where is mother? Where has mother gone?)

That would bring Manala, their grandmother, to the hut. Manala who had never forgiven her for being the woman in whom her son found the honey of the deep of night, woman's sweetness. Manala would take care of the children, the woman consoled herself: After all, they are her son's children. "Even though she doesn't like me," said the woman to herself, "she will have to look after them."

Her heart began to bleed. But the thorn saved her that pain: Ttssp — she remembered. I would not be a mother, if I didn't do this.

Past the kraal where a lone ram lay chewing cud; past the wide open gate that had not been closed even when as a *makoti*, a new wife, she had been carried into this home all those years ago; down the lane winding towards the river and past the brooding fields where maize stalks tall as a child of ten stood still in the airless night; and she had left her home.

Anyone who saw her now would know she was up to no good. She was a witch about her witchery, some would say. Others would call her a wanton, a slut who could not wait for her husband's return and had been spied on her way to meet her illicit lover. The more imaginative would surely give him substance: not a name but a more tantalizing form. Vague allusions are stronger than outright lies; no one can actually disprove them. And a few would put a stamp of authenticity on their tale by having seen, with their own eyes, this wicked woman locked in indelicate embrace with "I can't name names, you know whites put you in jail for that sort of thing." In the end, she knew they would say she ran away to hide a pregnancy that began too many moons after her husband had left. Her innocent mission, born of desperation, would give rise to tales she was glad she would not be there to hear.

Ttssp! Her children hungered, daily. Ttssp! Her husband was a dog that unsheathes itself onto a tuft of grass. He forgot the grass he'd peed on. Forgot what came from that. Ttssp-ttssp! Away the woman flew on her feet that hardly touched the ground, her blanket rolled and girded around her waist.

Down towards the river, she took the steep slope of the knoll; avoiding the gentler path. She did not feel her knees protest at the abuse as her calloused feet ground clods, ignored pebbles, and rebuffed razor-sharp stones.

Alongside the river she hurried, her step as swift as its flow; the swish swi-i-i-ss sshh of the water surged through her veins.

A night bird took umbrage at her invasion and with piercing cry flapped and winged away.

She reached the shallows with the fierce dark that precedes dawn. She spread her blanket; took off all her clothes and rolled them in the blanket into a careful bundle; and onto her head it went.

One hand holding firm her possessions, the other steadying her, slowly she waded across the cold, swirling water. The tide strong; she firmed her legs as she straddled those whirling, sucking gushes: her progress slowed by the need to fight the downdrift.

At last she had gained the other bank. Too wrapped in the heat the drop of blood gave her body, urging her on and on, not once had she thought of witches, as she fought to ford the river.

She paused to scan the horizon. She'd get real rest on the train. There was a field to cross, half grown with mealie stalks. She ploughed through.

Angry red blotches splashed the far sky as she came to the foot of the brooding high mountain. Up, she looked, high up to where the peak reached up and kissed the red-tinged sky. Soon, she was lost in the black thick of tree, shrub, and undergrowth.

The taste of the long trek dried her throat. Ttssp! The hunger she'd left behind spurred her flagging feet. She could smell it, the hunger gnawing at her children; gnawing at her heart. A dense dank plugged her nostrils: warm, wet, dying foliage giving birth to new soil.

The mountain pressed against her face, blacking all. She was as good as blind. The flurry of an upset nest gave her a start. But she did not stop. Then a large-sounding toad croaked, calling forth an eager, perky response from an attentive mate. Here and there, as the woman plodded on, things of the mountain night skulked away from the dawn.

Red softened to orange-gold and some soft touches of pink. Birds chirruped, hidden in bushes, and the night owl hooted, swishing low, slow wings towards his rest. The woman trudged on. Her nipples hardened from the milk wanting and waiting. She felt as if they belonged to another, as if she no longer knew why they burned.

In a gorge near the top she stumbled on a baboon dreaming away. Startled, he coughed his irritation as he lunged clumsily into the denser blackness. Imperceptibly, the air thinned, the mustiness fell from her nostrils. She crested the height.

Like an invading warrior, she surveyed the terrain. Bathed in soft hues of pink, even then paling to whitish pink turning to the hot white of an impatient sun, Umatata lay bare and silent; not a soul stirred in welcome or rejection.

Briefly she wondered whether any of her children had awakened. Was the baby, even then, crying for her feed? Was her mother-in-law already in the house with her children? Would she look after them? Or? . . . Or . . ? her thoughts refused to go any further. Instead, the thorn reminded her why she was doing what she was doing. If I don't, I would not be a mother: Ttssp!

The woman was ice-cold, drenched in sweat as she stood there drinking in the sprawl of the sleeping town at her feet.

Kneeling, she took out first the one then the other breast. Plumped hard and veined, they were hot to her crying hand. Squirt-squirt;

jets of white streamed to foam the ground. Squirt-squirt-squirt: the greedy soil quenched its thirst with her baby's life while near her knees the woman's eyes wet a spot.

Relieved, she put her breasts back beneath her tattered dress. One last look, the road was clear. One last sigh, for the children who sent her away, whose hunger drove her through night, river, field, forest, and mountain. How she loved them.

And a fresh drop of blood warmed her resolve anew. Her weary stride woke up, her body straightened from the slouch that had stolen over it. And although her eyes still did not sing, they dried themselves and looked right ahead. Her mind was made up. There was no going back.

2

Atini

I am Atini, though Mrs. Reed calls me Tiny. I have been working for Mrs. Reed for eighteen months now. And a mixed bag it has been too, if you ask me. I don't mind Mrs. Reed; she's not a bad medem at all. But then, I don't have that much experience of medems and my situation was so desperate any medem would have looked like my guardian angel, I suppose.

Well, a lot of the maids here would call Mrs. Reed a lot of things, in fact they do. But I doubt any would call her anything remotely resembling an angel. Most wouldn't even call her cousin to an angel. And I know not a few who have voiced sentiments that indicate she is nearer the other side of the scale, in their reckoning.

But me, my friend, I was destitute and the woman gave me a job. Some of the maids who work near me and who knew Imelda, the woman from whom I got the job, didn't like the way I got the job and tried to be funny to me; like they tried to show me their long faces and wouldn't greet me, or, if they didn't have enough guts to not greet me then they would give me a cold "hello"; not one tooth showing in smile. I just went on working as long as Mrs. Reed paid me and I could send my children money.

Sometimes, though, I wonder whether they had a good reason for not liking how I got the job? Did I do wrong? If so, would it have been less wrong to let my starving children go on starving and perhaps die?

Anyway, they have forgiven me now. At least I think they have, because they've taken to coming over to my room in the evenings. Funny thing though, it's never more than two at any one time. If one of them finds two already here, she'll either not stay or one of the two who were here before her will leave. I wonder why they do that? Really, these women of the town are not the same as the women in the village. I suppose I'll learn and be like them one day after I've been here long enough to forget the ways of the village.

They were kind to me when I first came and had nowhere to stay. I only knew Nombini who is from my village, and I hadn't even written to let her know I was coming. But then, when I didn't know I was coming until I left not knowing where I was going, how could I have let her know?

Once I'd found Nombini, she took me in and hid me in her room without her *mlungu* woman knowing I was there. They don't like that, the *mlungu* women, that the maid should keep someone in her room. They say that makes their own girl steal to feed the person in her room.

Nombini kept me in her room and the other maids helped her with food and clothes because I came naked. Nombini burned the clothes I arrived wearing; they had been rags when I left. After the journey, some of it on foot through forests and rivers, by the time I got here they were flenters — threads hanging onto each other with nothing really keeping them together. But, hey, my body was covered; and for that I thanked the Lord.

I had been here almost two months when Imelda had to go home to the village of Malenge in Mzimkhulu. Someone was very ill; I can't remember whether it was her mother or father. Her medem wouldn't let her leave unless she brought her another girl who would take her place. Imelda was so happy I wasn't working. It didn't matter to her that I had never worked and her medem was a fussy so-and-so and had told her: "And mind you don't bring me a *mampara*." Well sweetheart, I was more than a *mampara*. I didn't even know what a *mampara* was then, and that should show you what a *mampara* I was.

I think the only reason Mrs. Reed took me is that she cannot bear to think of herself without someone to do things for her. She doesn't know how to be without a maid and even a useless maid, to her, is better than none at all.

After a week, however, she started showing me her smile. I knew she liked how I worked. I was careful to do everything the way Imelda had shown me. And, of course, I got a lot of help from Mrs. Reed: "This way, Tiny," she'd say, showing me how she wanted something done. I think that first week she almost did all the work herself while she was busy showing me.

Imelda had asked for three weeks from Mrs. Reed. She had told me she would be gone for a full month, maybe even a month and a half. But I don't think it would have made any difference what she'd told Mrs. Reed. As I said, by the end of the first week, Mrs. Reed was happy with my work. She was so happy, in fact, she paid me almost double what she paid Imelda. "You are a very neat worker, Tiny. You work clean," she said, giving me the money.

Oh, the Tiny comes from my name, Atini. I feel funny being called Tiny; I am a large woman. *Sidudla*, that is a name people give to a fat person who cannot even pretend she isn't fat. But Mrs. Reed said: "Oh, I can't say your names, they're difficult. All those clicks and things. I'll call you Tiny." And so, I became Tiny; fat as I am. Terrible, the things one does without even planning them. God is my witness, I never wanted to take anybody's job. By the end of the second week, Mrs. Reed was busy making me feel sorry for her. She would be telling me, all the time, about what a good girl I was and how she was so happy to have me and would pay me well. She didn't say, right out, she didn't want Imelda back. But I knew that was what she was saying although she was not saying it. And she knew I knew.

Friend, by the time poor Imelda came back, a whole eleven weeks after she'd left, even I couldn't see how she could expect her job back. Where would her job have been if I'd left and found myself another? Wouldn't Mrs. Reed have hired someone else then? So, we'd both saved ourselves the trouble and stayed with each other, Mrs. Reed and I.

I'd be a hairy liar if I said I had any misgivings about getting much better wages than Imelda had received. I accepted the extra as my due. I believed I worked clean as Mrs. Reed said. And when she asked me: "Tiny, do you have another job to go to when Imelda returns?" I had told her the naked truth. "No, medem." As my heart smiled in anticipation.

Of course Imelda saw the whole thing in a different light; selfish, insensitive woman:

"I got you that job to stand in for me, not to take it from me," she growled.

"But you stayed away longer than you said you would. And if I'd left you'd have lost it anyway." I also reminded her she had said she might not want the job, in fact, upon her return and I would be more than welcome to it.

"Atini, my sister, let that white woman go find her own maid. Don't do this to me. How can you?" This she said in Xhosa, our mother tongue, a language the likes of Mrs. Reed had never bothered learning.

She was standing outside, Mrs. Reed, talking to her through the door opened only a crack. She could see me behind her employer's back, standing there wearing her uniform several sizes too small for me.

I heard desperation in her voice. She really, really wanted — NO, needed, this job. But then, what about me? Anyway, Mrs. Reed had scrapped the last twinge of doubt from me when she said: "Whether you stay or not, I am not having Imelda back." It had not been a strong doubt; and it died an easy death. "Talk to your medem," I said to Imelda. "If she wants you, I am not stopping you from getting your job back."

What purpose would be served by the two of us treading Desperation Street? So, I stayed with Mrs. Reed. And Imelda went around painting my name black as crow.

At first the other girls took her part; finding fault with me. Even my home-girl, Nombini, told me she was ashamed of what I had done, stabbing Imelda in the back like that. I felt really bad, really bad. But, what could I do? I stayed put and worked for my starving children whom I'd deserted while they trustingly slept. I kept reminding myself that my children woke up to find me gone one morning; that they hadn't known where I was or what had happened to me until I sent word when I found someone returning to the village. I reminded myself I had not left my children to come to help maids who couldn't keep their jobs stay in those jobs. *Awu!* If Imelda had done her work well, why would this *mlungu* woman have told her she did not want her? *I-iish!* I told myself, Atini, forget the whole thing — who likes you and who does not. Remember your children and work for them; you didn't come here to look for friends.

When they saw their ignoring me didn't bother me at all, one by one they started talking to me: one by one.

Now, I have to be careful I don't find myself in another soup. Women like talking about each other and then forget they said what, and before you know it you will be answering questions about what you said to whom about whom. I have no time for that. But I would be lying if I said their stories are uninteresting.

Indeed, I am learning a lot about this place: the white women, their likes and dislikes. Which of the *mlungu* men chase after the servants. Who treats their servants with some respect. I am learning about ourselves too, the maids.

We sit here in my room and, because I am the newest maid, each one of my neighbors is helpful in letting me know what's what: like what my medem is like, really like and compared to their own; which woman I should be careful of after I find a boyfriend; which one has not yet learnt the difference between give and lend when it comes to another's money; who drinks more than is good for them (of course, those who do not drink at all tell me who drinks, period).

But, of all the stories I like, the ones that show me in much better light than Imelda are the best. And boy, are there stories about her! That is what happens when you go around painting other people's names black. It all comes back to you. Yes, indeed, we do reap what we sow. Of course, I hear a lot of the things she went around telling other people about me, most not true, as can be imagined. But then, it looks like she was one to spin tales about others: maids, medems, their husbands, boyfriends, and secret lovers. Imelda knew everybody's business and had a chest that had been kicked wide open by a horse. Couldn't keep a thing to herself, that one. Things just spilled out of her chest. I am even hearing tales about maids who were here long ago and whom I am most unlikely to encounter. A whole new world is opening right in front of my eyes.

3

Stella

"Saw your medem's car drive off. Guess she's off to her self-defense class? Thought I'd pop over. Put the kettle on, girl. You know my Goat Food Woman, the fridge is full of leaves, seeds, growing things, and smelly rotting things. The milk is from beans, she tells me. Beans. I wasn't raised by people who milk beans. Beans have teats? Hey, if we're not careful, one of these days these strange women we work for will feed us snakes and frogs I tell you.

"There, the kettle is boiling. We have no tea or coffee in that house: 'Those are drugs, Stella,' my medem tells me. But my head tells me something else.

"Thank you, sure smells good. Thank you. If I had the money, I'd buy myself at least coffee and put it in my room.

"I don't know why I go on working for such a sour *suurlemoen* of a woman, you know? Believe me, I know we say a lot of bad things about Stork Legs, your medem, but at least with her, you know where you stand. Not that change-face so-and-so I work for.

"I'm sure you've seen her with her always-mouth-open-face: she could win a Mrs. Sunshine Sweetest Smile Competition; couldn't she? Always cheerful she looks, hey? Don't be fooled. I could tell you things about that woman — things you would never believe.

"Gets me downright mad to think of the way she has used me over the years. But, I get even. I pay her back; and then some more.

"She wipes her sunshine smile away when she talks to me and she wants to tell me something she knows is not nice.

"'Stella,' she will say Thursday lunchtime, 'can you please be back for dinner? I'm having visitors tonight.'

"Now, tell me that is not cruel. Here's a woman who has seven days a week like everybody else. When does she choose to entertain? On the one evening a week she knows her maid is off. And her smile is there for everyone to see how kind she is.

"From the word go, I knew there was something not nice about this woman I work for. First day here, what do I find? There's her bath tub full of water. The same water she's just had a bath in. Her dirty water. Dirty from her own body. It is too dirty for her to put her hand in and pull the plug out. Can you believe that? This woman would leave her bath water for me to let it out?

"I'm not saying she should wash the tub. Hey, she's paying me to do that — OK. But, you mean she can't let out her own, own water?

"And, if you think that's all I found in that tub you're wrong. There, swimming, afloat in that water of hers, was her panty . . . she'd left it in there for me to wash.

"What! Me? I taught her a lesson, that very first day. I took something, a peg, I think, and lifted that panty of hers and put it dripping wet, to the side of the bath which I then cleaned until it was shiny-shiny.

"You think she got my message? Wrong. Doesn't she leave me a note: 'Stella, wash the panty when you wash the bath.'

"What do you mean what did I do? I did not go to school for nothing. I found a pen in her bookshelf and found a piece of paper and wrote her a note too:

"'Medem,' I said in the note, 'please excuse me but I did not think anyone can ask another person to wash their panty. I was taught that a panty is the most intimate thing . . . my mother told me no one else should even see my panty. I really don't see how I can be asked to wash someone else's panty.'

"That was the end of that panty nonsense. You see, she leaves the house very early. And at that time I worked sleep-out for her so we used to write a lot of messages for each other.

"And then every Sunday she's off to Church. Hypocrites, these white people are. Real hypocrites. Never practice what they preach.

"She goes to Church every Sunday, but when Master isn't here, you should see what goes on in this place. Then, she comes home early from work: 'Stella, you can take the rest of the day off.'

"What am I supposed to do with a half day off I didn't know I was getting? You think I have money to be running up and down for nothing? But, that doesn't worry Sunshine Smile. All she wants is that there's no maid to see her business. Hypocrite and *skelm* on top of it too.

"But me, I take the check out of her. I take the half day off she gives me. But I stay right here in my room and give myself a rest.

"And she doesn't know I need to rest. She thinks I am a donkey that can go on and on working. When I'm off, do you know she can think nothing of giving me a whole suitcase full of clothes. Don't think she's like other medems who give their girls their old clothes. Not this one, my friend. She wants me to sell those clothes for her.

"'Here Stella,' the smile is bigger than the whole sky, 'I'm sure your friends in Langa would like these clothes. Almost new.'

"That's the woman I work for. It is not enough I work for her six to six, six days a week. On my half day off I must be working for her. Selling her second-hand clothes. She even pins the price on each one.

"Now don't think these almost new clothes have been drycleaned. You think she'd spend her money like that? There, I must carry clothes smelling her smell, carry them home and sell them to my friends. Of course, the one's the donkey can wash, those she sees to it that they *are* washed and ironed. She's not stingy with my strength, oh no!

"Then she'll take one of these clothes, look at it like it was a child going away, and say — 'Take this one for yourself.' That is how she pays me for carrying a heavy suitcase, making my friends laugh at me selling her silly clothes. You know, sometimes I just save myself the trouble, take the clothes and pay her the money — bit by bit —

until I've paid all of it. Then, when I find someone going back to the village, I send the clothes to my relatives there.

"You don't think you would be sick working for someone like this — making you work like a donkey and feeding you goat food? She really gets on my nerves. But I must be careful. If there's one thing that makes her out and out mad at me, it's when I'm sick.

"My sickness she never understands. She thinks I'm made of stone. She can be sick and when she's sick I must run all over the place making her feel good: 'Turn the TV on. Turn the TV off. Make me black tea. Warm me some milk. I want dry toast. Give me the magazine. Go get me the newspaper. I forgot, *Cosmopolitan* is out. Take all calls and write down the messages. Is that Joan? I'll take the call.'

"But I must never get sick. 'You think I run a clinic here, my girl?' That's what she says first day I'm sick. Day number two: 'Maybe you should go home and send one of your daughters to help.'

"You know this woman has children the same ages as mine. I must send my children here to help her and her children while I'm sick. My children must miss school to come and make sure their goat food is made, the beds are made, their shoes are polished, their clothes are washed.

"I also discovered she doesn't like me to be sick and stay here. I think she believes my sickness will jump onto them and kill them all. It's all right for me to catch their germs when they are sick. But my germs — that's a different story.

"Ho! White people! You slave for them. Slave for their children. Slave for their friends. Even slave for their cats and dogs. And they thank you with a kick in the back.

"Anyway, I must go, I'm making yogurt bread over there, the dough must be ready by now. Hey, thanks for the coffee — now, I'm really awake."

4

Sheila

"Did I wake you up? You weren't already asleep, surely? A young woman like you, you should go out a bit, you know. Then again, what nonsense am I talking . . . when would you go out since this woman you work for keeps you in her kitchen so late. What time did you knock off tonight?

"Let me tell you something — this *mlungu* woman of yours, she's a real she-dog, this one. Can't keep a maid; changes maids faster than other medems change their stockings. Every day you look, there's a new girl hanging up the washing in this yard. Sometimes a girl's gone before the maids from around here have even had a chance to get to know her name. How long have you been here now? A month?

"Whaaat! More? My God, she should throw a party. I don't know how many girls, except the last one . . . that one stayed with her a long time . . . I don't know how many girls leave her by the end of the first month. And some have left even before that; many leaving their money behind too.

"You laugh? I'm serious as the back of pajamas. Ask her for a raise. You should. A month with a woman like the one you're working for is like a year in another kitchen. The woman really eats up maids.

"Tell me, how much is she paying you? No, tell me. I can tell you if that's what she paid the last girl she had. She's funny that way; her wage jumps up and down all the time. I think she looks at a girl first and thinks to herself — 'Aha! this is a *plaasjapie* . . . straight from the bundus. Knows nothing about money. She's never seen more than one ten rand note at a time.' If that's what she thinks of the girl, 'strue's God, that *arme* girl will not get more than two hundred rands a month from her.

"That's what she's paying you, isn't it? I'm sure it is. Since you're so shy and you're young, she'll say you have no experience; and then start to rob you, paying you peanuts.

"That's something else, hey? *Blerry* cheek! What do these white women think they mean — no experience. Do they suppose we eat our food raw?

"You know, these women really take themselves a bit seriously, don't you say?

"So, she'll say you've no experience and pay you chicken feed. Is she going to send you to school to get experience for washing her dirty clothes? Does she teach you how to iron her husband's shirts? Can she show you how to cook?

"They're so *lekker* useless with their big mouths you know, they make me laugh. And then they have the cheek to *nogal* say we are dirty. Where would they be without us forever cleaning after them so they can be clean? Pray to God up high, my dear, you never have the bad luck to get a job where there was no maid for more than a week. You'll see then who is clean or not. One day, two days without a maid, and they start to stink. The whole place stinks inside a week; even if they buy those cans of air freshener stuff. That has no hands like the maid. All it can do is just dye the air; and the smells just laugh HA HA HA; like, what the hell's going on? Who you think is frightened of your silly air freshener stuff? No, my dear, nothing can make the white people clean like the maid does. But, of course, they can't say we are the ones responsible for them being clean. They never give us our due; but never mind, we know what's what. And that's what is important.

"Mine knows all the complaints: I'm sure she reads them from a book. She's always reading. That's how she got her eyes condemned, you know. Without her thick glasses, she can't see her own finger if she holds it up right in front of her own face. But my mistakes, ooh, *that* she sees very, very clearly, my friends. She is always complaining about everything:

"'You didn't fold the carpet back to sweep underneath it.'

"'You left the washing outside too long; you'll have to damp it now before you iron it.'

"'Did you rinse these glasses? You must always rinse dishes otherwise we are eating soap with our food. And, another thing, you didn't get the eyes out of the potatoes you cooked last night. Use the back of the potato peeler, the pointed end, you know? That's why it's there.'

"One *shushu* day, when I'm nice and well-done fed up, I'm going to tell her to her face: 'Do it and let me see how you want it done. Show me.'

"And watch her burn her hands or cut a finger off — if it's my lucky day. She doesn't know the front side of the iron. That will shut her big mouth and give my hot ears a rest.

"But, at least, she pays me decent, more or less. For this area, I mean. The women in this area don't pay that much. If you want good wages, you should go and work in Cape Town, in Constantia or Camps Bay or Llandudno. And then you will not see another maid until you are on the bus on your off days. But the women there pay a lot because they know it's too far and their maids see only the baboons. So you get paid for living with *mlungus* and baboons, six days a week.

"Have you heard about how maids should not let the white women call them girls or servants anymore? And we should join a group to fight for our rights? Do you think that can happen? White women can learn not to call us girl? After all these years they're used to calling us anything they like — never mind if the girl likes it or not; never mind if it's her name or not? Do you really think they'll learn that? Me, myself, I don't think so. I really don't think so.

"Of course, I think it's a great idea. We should have maids' groups. The women we work for *must* have their groups too. Otherwise, if they don't have groups all over the place, how do they know how much they pay us? They talk about these things, the white women. They tell each other what to do about maids. Only we're too dumb to see they do this and control us. You can't even change your job because the next medem is just like the one you're running away from. They treat us the same because they know what that same is.

"'You can ask around if you want, ask any girl around here, you won't get higher wages.' How can the woman say that if she is not sure? If she is sure, ask yourself, how can she know so much what the other medems in the area pay their girls? They talk about us, about how much to pay us, what food to give us, I tell you, we are their number one problem. If they talked so much about their children, they would not have the spoilt wild animals we have to look after. But no, they must talk about our pay.

"You want to laugh? Let me tell you how much the woman I work for pays me. After eight years. Eight years. And when I complain she tells me, 'Go ask the girl next door how much Mrs. Van Niekerk pays her. Go. And she's been with them twenty years.' How does she know . . . since these white women don't visit and chat to one another as we do?

"But yours, yours, my dear, is something else. Her stingy is not the everyday kind of stingy. Her stingy is a sickness. You know something? She even sells her old clothes to her maid. Be careful if she gives you anything. Make sure she is giving it to you not selling it. One of the maids before you ended up in jail. Three months' wages she owed your medem. Three months of her sweat. And she is quick to call the police, that woman of yours. Watch your step with her.

"If you refuse to pay for something — clothing you didn't even know you were buying or a plate you broke by mistake: one-two-three, the police van will be at that house. Four-five-six: you'll be in the police cell.

"You know the police won't even let you open your dirty mouth. You think they'll let a kaffir maid say the white medem is lying? Anyone who thinks that is mad or blind. Be careful of her. Careful. She's a real snake in the grass.

"She also goes to the maid's room when you are not here: off. She wants to see if you've stolen her things. Listen to that, hey! Isn't she full of nonsense? Don't think she'll come to your room because something is missing from her house. Oh, no. She'll come to your room to see if she can find something there that she thinks shouldn't be there; something too expensive for you to buy. Then, of course, she knows you stole it since she knows she pays you only so much and you can't pay for things that cost that much more than she pays you. Her suspicion was right. She finds a nice thing in your room — except, it is not hers. You have nothing of hers in your room.

"Don't think that is the end of the story.

"Now, she has to think about where you stole the thing from. If not from her, then from whom? She can't worry herself thinking since she was wrong when she came to your room to see what you stole from her that maybe you didn't steal anything from anyone. No. She isn't going to say to herself: '*Ag, Here God*, maybe I'm wrong. maybe my *arme* girl's not a common thief. Maybe she's a decent girl and I am wrong.' No. She'll say: 'Okay, this is not mine. But this girl didn't buy it. Now, where did she steal it from?'

"All these women we work for, they all think we are thieves, finish *en klaar*. Nothing but thieves. All of us. All of them think like that. but yours goes right into your room behind your back and she *kraps* around there while you're away visiting your people in Duncan Village.

"Did you say you have a little one? *Ag tog*; what is it? Oo, *foeitog, die arme skepsel*, mus' miss you a lot, hey? Cries when you go away on your off-days, neh? *Ja!* It's a shame they made a law so now you can't bring your baby to stay with you where you work. Used to be like that when I had little ones. Mind you, it was a lot of work. You were like working two jobs at the same time; minding your own and the medem's and then all the other work also, hey. But I think it was still better that way. Now, you have to pay someone else to look after your baby. And you can't always be sure they're doing a good job either, hey? It's a shame.

"I was telling you how much I get after eight years with this woman, mmh? And only January this year, too, she tell me . . . 'Oh, master say yes, we can afford to give you a little extra, my girl.'

"Big thing. She talk about it from New Year's Day already. Talk. Talk. Talk. Until I can't wait to see what this 'extra' looks like. I'm like a child waiting for a Christmas box. I wait for this January end of the month, all excited. I wait and wait and wait. Well, let me tell you something, two month-ends are slower than a blind, cripple, fat old man: end December and end January. Those two are always trouble end of the months. You know why? 'Cos, you're *mos platsak* broke from buying all the Christmas *lekker goed* and then come the school fees and the *blerry* school uniforms. You see how one dress never last for more than a year? These uniforms! They make them like that, you know, from the factory. They don't want them to last 'cos if they last, where're they going to get their money from? *Skelms*, the whole shoot: teachers, principals, inspectors; they all get a share from the factory. The school buys so many uniforms this year, they get so much from the money the factory or wholesale make. Who pays for their 'scrub my back, I'll scrub yours?' We poor domestic servants . . . Listen to me; here I'm the first to forget I'm not a servant anymore. I am a worker; I must remember that. I'm just as bad as these white women, hey? Can't teach an old dog new tricks, as they say: heh?

"Juslike! Look at the time. You know what I came here to tell you? Tomorrow night, we're all meeting at Sophie's kitchen. You know Sophie? Down by the Greek café at the corner of this street and Lover's Walk. Her medem is the crazy one who lets us use her house for our meetings. No wonder she is always in trouble with the government.

"Anyway, that is where we are meeting tomorrow night. Nine-thirty sharp. And don't let this woman keep you away from the meeting. Tell her early in the morning, before she comes with her own nonsense about what she wants you to do for her in the evening, tell her you have to take food money to your baby as soon as you've done the dishes.

"In fact, let me phone you in the morning; mine goes bowling at ten. After I put the phone down she will ask: 'Who was that?' They always want to know who was that when you get a phone call. Then, you can tell her it was the woman who looks after the baby telling you she has run out of baby food.

"She'll let you knock off early then, maybe eight or half-past eight. Don't waste time then, rush over to my place and you can wait there till it's time to go to the meeting. If you wait here, she'll suspect something. And then she'll find something you didn't finish or didn't do well. That's the trick they always use to get a girl back into the kitchen in the middle of the night.

"My dear, I must go and let you go back to sleep. Can you imagine what we'll feel like tomorrow morning when our alarms go.

"One last thing — and then I really must leave you. Let me give you a tip. Friend, don't listen to anything the other maids tell you about the woman you work for. Or her husband. Sometimes people tell you things and it's because they're jealous, that's all. These maids here are full of rubbish. You just go on doing your work — keep your mouth shut. And when they tell you things — listen with one ear only. Many will be wanting the same — the very same thing they will tell you: 'Don't do that.' You listen to me.

"Hey, if you don't let me go, your alarm will start to ring and I'll still be here. Let me run."

5

Sophie

"*Wethu!* Why didn't you come to the meeting last night? My *mlungu* woman has been asking me about that the whole morning. You know how she is — for her, whether she's at the Advice Office or back here in the house, it is all the same. She must be putting her nose in everybody's business.

"I told her you said you were coming and I didn't know why you hadn't showed up. 'Are you going to find out? Or shall I?' she asks, knowing I don't like her talking to all the maids and their medems. That is how she ends up asking me things I don't want to talk to her about; and she gets me into trouble with the medems of these women. You would think a *mlungu* woman wouldn't worry herself about maid gossip: not the one I work for, *hay'mntakwethu*.

"How is Legs of a Bird these days? I hope she's sick and tired of changing girls. We are sick and tired of seeing new faces from her kitchen everyday. But I think you use your head; I think you're going to stay with her, never mind her nonsense. That's good. You must just think of your children.

"You know something? I think medem is worried your *mlungu* woman will mess you up the same way she messed up Imelda. You know Imelda can't take? That is why that nice young man who works at Groote Schuur Hospital changed his mind about marrying her. He had already sent his people to her people and they were talking *lobola* business.

"But he was worried. They had been trying to have a child. A long time they tried and tried. But no, she could not take. Witchdoctor after witchdoctor couldn't help Imelda. And you see, seeing she'd been pregnant before (that was before this man) she knew she could take. And the man has a child already. So he knew he was well. They tried and tried and tried. But no, Imelda couldn't take.

"A white doctor finally told them what's what:

"'When were you last pregnant?' he asks her.

"'*Hanana-hanana; hanana-hanana*,' . . . Imelda is all over the place. Remember, the boyfriend-nearly-husband has not heard anything about — 'Hey, by the way, once I was nearly a mother.' Mmh? But only then did Imelda see the truth; see what had been done to her by her medem's doctor.

"That doctor her medem had taken her to when she had stopped, that doctor cleaned up Imelda. Cleaned her up not only for what was inside her then — but for all those that would have lain inside her in time to come.

"What could the poor man do after hearing that? What else did he want her for? If he'd wanted a bull he'd have bought himself one.

"My medem believes your medem is the worst medem because of that. Mind you, the woman I work for sees little good in medems — in white people generally. I tell you, that woman is a person, a human being although she is white. She feels for another person.

"You know she bought me the house I live in in Mdantsane? Mmhh? Do you know that? And this is not my mother's child I'm talking about. She is not my sister but a *mlungu* woman I just work for, that's all. But she buys a house for me. How many medems would do a thing like that for their girls? How many?

"Of course I pay for her being so nice to me. Oo, my friend, do I pay. You think a person who walks on two feet can do so much for you for nothing? Didn't the Indian man at the shop tell us: 'Naasing for naasing and very littel forahh siiling?'

"I have a beautiful house with electric and hot water; but my shoulders and my knees are always burning: Work. Work. Work. I work until I drop dead each day. *Whuwoo!* Get her money right out of my shoulders and my knees? That, she does. Oh, yes, that she does.

"Hey, I haven't seen Nombini for a while. How is she? What do you mean you don't know? I thought you two were cousins. No?

"I'm surprised she doesn't come here to your room every day. Nombini is a born manager, you know. She should have been a teacher or had twelve children of her own and a husband who earned enough so she could be with the children all the time, bossing them.

"You didn't let her push you around, I see. That must be why she is not in and out of your room telling you what to do and what not to do. Right?

"Actually, now I remember someone, Stella I think it was, telling me only last week that Nombini had told her she had learned her lesson; she would never help anybody again because here she'd harbored you and now you were choosing other maids as friends.

"You know what I said to Stella? I said, 'I bet you my fish and chips on Saturday, Tiny didn't let Nombini treat her like her first born.'

"I know Nombini by now. If you don't say yes to everything she wants you to do, you are no good, she'll say. To her, friend means 'my sheep that follows me everywhere I go, does my bidding, and asks no questions.'

"For a long time she used to bully me too. Not any more. Medem called her and scolded her. She told her to leave me alone or there'd be big trouble.

"How are your children? Did you manage to bring the younger ones you say you are worried about? Shame.

"Good news: Sylvia has found a Saturday afternoon char. And it pays well. That she-dog she works for pays her pocket money, as you know. But the good thing is that because she doesn't want to be feeding her over the weekend she gives Sylvia Saturday afternoon and all of Sunday off.

"Now, Sylvia has a job, Saturday afternoons. Fifteen rand, just for the afternoon. I told her not to take the money until month end.

Sixty rands for four Saturdays. Isn't that good money? Really, students pay better and fuss less. These women we work for treat us like dogs, worse than their dogs, in fact. That is, most of them.

"I feel so bad when I complain about mine because she really is a good, good person. All the other girls complain about real things — real problems which are big. Their medems pay them little. They don't give them enough rest; one hour every day, half a day each week, and only two weeks of holiday for the year. I get all those things.

"Am I not the one all the other girls envy? 'Oh, Sophie, God loves you, my dear. How did you get a *mlungu* woman who is so-oo good?' I listen to those words and my heart tells me there is truth in them.

"I can't complain like the other girls: I get good wages. When I have trouble at home, if she knows about it, she does something to help. She's cross if I don't tell her my troubles. So, you see, I really shouldn't complain.

"I tell myself I should understand her side when she's cross — like if I'm late. I can be late if she's not going anywhere or if she's not having people over. But if my lateness makes her look bad, then she could boil me alive.

"I have a good medem; that is the truth. But when she brings the whole Duncan Village here to dinner — and I must cook and wash dishes up to nine at night, then I complain in my heart.

"I complain very much although I say nothing to her. I complain because I don't know why she has to make me serve people who are black just like me. It is a punishment, I feel.

"I am a maid and they are teachers, and nurses, and social workers, and so forth. So what! I leave the location and its people and I come to work in a white woman's kitchen. And there she takes her *kombi*; takes it and goes to the location to bring it right back here to her kitchen. Is she going to serve this whole location she brings here? No. The maid is there. Now, I am a maid to serve black people.

"I am not saying she shouldn't like all people. But, really, it's not fair to make me sweat for people who are just as poor as I am. Not one of these people has ever given me a tip. Not a single one. White people tip. Black people just sit there and eat and eat and eat. I'm lucky if *one* says 'thank you' to the cook. No manners, even if they are educated.

"I sometimes get so angry I think of leaving this woman. But she bought me a house, a beautiful house in Mdantsane. It has carpet on the floor. It has a real bathroom; a bathroom I can use. How do you leave a *mlungu* woman who has bought a house for you?

"I feel the house is cement; because of it I can never leave this woman. Cement is like that. Never put your feet deep into wet cement. If you do, make sure you get it out before the cement dries. My cement has dried and both my feet are in this woman's house. I am stuck — for the rest of my life. But, I shouldn't complain.

"I have a house; my very own house. How many of us can say that; including the educated ones? Even after a long life of hard work every day — how many of us can say: I have a house and it is mine?

"When I think of just that, I am ashamed I complain in my heart. Even if medem doesn't hear me complain, I shouldn't complain: it is not right that I do. This woman is too good to me.

"I feel sorry not more white people are like medem. But there are so few good white people that the bad ones swallow them and we don't see the good ones. And then we forget they are there."

6

Virginia

"Bad luck comes in threes, people say. I got all three yesterday, my sister.

"First, I'm clearing up after breakfast when the stupid cat rubs itself against my leg; making me drop a plate. Is this bad luck or what? You tell me. And first thing in the morning too.

"Five rands from my wages, end of the month. And you know Tracer doesn't forget — that's why she was called Tracer by the girls who worked for her before me. She traces every wrong thing back to the girl. Five rands: tell me how I'm paying rent in the location. Or maybe I'll pay rent and buy less food. Then will my children eat sand?

"Bad luck number two: I've been working for this woman five years now. Do you know what she tells me today? *Yhuu*!

"Maybe I should go and see a witchdoctor. Really, jokes aside, maybe someone is trying to make this woman chase me away so she can get my job. Where do you hear a woman tell me I stink? Me? Five years I work for this woman. Today, she discovers I smell.

"With my lunch, that is what I got from my medem today. I'm taking my plate to my room — just after I finish the dishes when I hear her say: 'Here, Virginia, take this for yourself, and use it.'

"When I look to see what she's giving me; *tyhini!* the woman is holding Sunlight soap and Mum — the cream. She must see my eyes are asking her 'Why?' Me, I say nothing with my own mouth. I just look at the things in her hands.

"'I'm sure you sweat a lot with the kind of work you are doing. I'm not saying you don't wash or anything like that.'

"I look at her and say nothing. I'm thinking to myself: After all these years I have worked for her; lived here with her; this woman has now traced all the bad smells in her house to my body?

"I took the things from her hand and put them right there on her window-sill, above the sink. They can stay there until they grow roots. She will see them get flowers, right there in her kitchen.

"If it wasn't for my pass, I'd leave this mad, mad woman. She is no good. No good at all. She has a bad heart: a heart that cannot feel for other people.

"I tell you, my sister, I lost all my appetite for that food. I put my plate in my room, took off my apron, my cap, and the slippers. I put on my sandals and went out. I didn't even ask myself where I was going. I just went out.

"And then on the Main Road I meet your Imelda. Didn't someone tell me she works in Nahoon? What is she doing so far away from where she works?

"You know, when you're used to somebody you don't see her bad points. Before she asked me how I was she was already asking me about you: Who visits you? Who are your friends among the maids here? Are you still with Mrs. Walk-on-Arms? How much is she paying you?

"I tell you, the only thing she didn't ask me about you is the color of your panties. But me, you know me, I told her nothing.

"That was my bad luck number three: meeting Imelda. Now she wants to blame everybody for losing her job here. Do you know how this same Imelda used to talk bad about poor Bird Legs? She would tell us she hated working for those people because they were dirty inside, in their hearts, and they think she is not only a slave but a she-dog. And today, she forgets all those things, changes her mind and wants to work for them.

"You just go on working there. They were not married. When you work for a woman, you're not married to her. She can always change her girls if she wants to; she is the one who is paying.

"All the girls are happy Imelda's gone; I can tell you that, my sister. Do you want to know how many girls she still owes money? That woman! She was a crook, a first class crook. Always borrowing money and telling you stories when the time to pay comes.

"I don't know how many times someone has died in that woman's family. There can't be many people left; she is running out of relatives.

"At first I used to give her money. You know that's our insurance — helping one another. We can't go to the bank when we're short of money: Ha! ha! ha! We don't go to the bank at all anyway. What would we do there? Put five rands in today — take it out tomorrow? The bank people would probably chase us away with our silly cents. Ha!

"And you know how I make extra money: stay in. All the women around here know Virgie is Ever-Ready for stay-in jobs. If their maid is off, is sick, can't stay in — for whatever reason — Virginia is always there. That's what I do to get a little more money. I don't steal it from my sisters, women sweating whole day long like me. I don't go to them telling them stories so they can give me their money and then I can't pay them. I do stay-in jobs — every day. And you know what? Some of these cheap medems — you know what they do to me? 'Virginia, my girl, just do this little ironing while you're here instead of sitting doing nothing the whole evening.'

"Can you believe that? You are staying in for the children. But because the woman's paying you, she wants you to work on top of it. They think watching their children is easy; they think it is peanut butter or jam; it is not work. That's what they think. Shows you how much they know their children.

"A girl just sits there for all the time they're out; she just sits there having a nice time. And they say to themselves: 'Why are we paying her to sit and enjoy herself in our nice house, looking after our nice children.' Ho-ho! I wish *they* would stay in. But then they wouldn't see anything anyway even if they did that. The children would be good because it is the blackness in us that makes the white children not to respect us. They can't help it; they learn that from their parents. Where have you seen the children of the crab crawling straight? Children learn from their parents.

"That's white women for you. Watching their children, losing your rest and your sleep, getting all the cheek from their children: and they think you are having a nice time. They are the ones who are dancing and you are watching their children. But they fix it in their minds that it is you who is having a nice time. One rand an hour, they pay you; and they are angry because they are paying you to have a nice time. I tell you, me? I will not be surprised one day if a white woman wants me to pay her because she let me stay in her beautiful house and spend time with her good children.

"White women are quick to see the favor they do for you but they never see any favor you do for them. Mine is always reminding me how she got my pass right. Now, in her eyes, I will die on my knees scrubbing her floors. Fixing my pass was buying me; that's what she thinks. Because she fixed my pass she can do anything bad — I can't leave her. She can pay me less money than all the other girls here — I am the lucky one: 'Who fixed your pass for you, my girl?' That's her answer to anything I say when I'm complaining.

"ONE DAY! One day I will remind her it was not her who had to spread her legs for that white dog, the Bantu Inspector who made my pass right. I think she forgets that.

"Me, I pull hard for my money, my dear; it doesn't rain down on me from the clouds. And then people like your friend, Imelda, just stretch out their hands and think you should just put your money there and then forget about it.

"Has your medem asked you to stay in? I used to stay in a lot for them; before Imelda worked there. They pay well for stay-in. If you can't do it, remember: Virgie — Ever-Ready. I know the girls say a lot of nonsense about your master. They say he tries tricks on the maids.

"Now, that, I don't know anything about. And people should be careful what they say. They shouldn't say things if they have no proof;

they'll go to jail, lying about white people. And there is a law about what they say that man is doing. You go around saying a person is breaking the law. Can you prove it? No? Then, watch your mouth; that is what I say. Watch your mouth. Remember, your mouth is your policeman. It can take you to jail."

7

Joyce

"My mother got me this job, but believe me, I'm not going to be a maid for long.

"I was a student doing matric. But since the riots, there have been no real classes. So Mother said: 'Ntombi, go to work until this thing is over and then you'll go back to school.'

"Do you know how many African women doctors there are? In this whole country? Five. FIVE — that's all!

"Well, look at me. Look at me real well. Look! There will be six — that, I promise you.

"I look at the people I work for. I look at them and I feel sorry for them, you know. The days of masters and medems with lots of slaves are going. Friend, before long, these people will learn to cook for themselves, clean for themselves, and scrub their own floors and do their laundry for themselves.

"This exploitation of the masses will stop. Its days are numbered. Workers are going to be paid a decent wage. Have you ever seen a non-white loaf of bread? Can you go and buy black milk? Does the price of cheese drop when a black person is buying it? It's fine to have cheap labor. But fodder costs the same whether the horse chewing it is black or white.

"Antie Sophie's medem is right in some ways. Domestic workers should work civilized hours like all other workers. They should be able to live with their families. And it should be a crime to pay a full-grown woman less than the pocket-money you give to your twelve-year-old.

"She is also right, the domestic worker should improve herself. But I don't agree with her idea of what that improvement means.

"Thank you, very much, but I don't want to learn to iron starched shirts better. I don't want to learn the ways of laying the most attractive table. I feel no woman should be condemned to life in another's kitchen.

"There ought to be a law — that no one serves as a maid for more than ten years unless they get certification that they are mentally impaired and there is no hope of rehabilitation.

"Only beyond-repair mental invalids should be domestic servants for all their working life. And the medem should be held responsible for the advancement of her maid — that should go hand in hand with the privilege of being served.

"And the color of the maid should not automatically be black. White women and men of all colors should be liberated enough and secure enough that they take jobs as domestic workers. This should not be the preserve of black women only. Neither should the position of master and medem: blacks too should experience those positions. We all need to expand, to grow, to stretch out and be free. We must stop living according to prescription.

"You tell me of the kind white women who buy books for the children of their maids. But, aren't these maids working women? Why do they need to have someone else pay for their children's books? And, why do the white women feel compelled to buy books for children who are not theirs? Could it be that somewhere in their foggy consciences there are vague disturbances? Could it be that they themselves are not fully convinced of the adequacy of the wage they offer their employees? If that is the case, even half the case, then buying books is hardly the answer.

"Surely, even in the minds of people who have long forgotten what it is to be without blinders, white women must see they do not pay their servants a living wage or an adequate wage: to say nothing of a fair wage. That can only come from a just medem or master.

"The white woman can do all sorts of things for her maid. She can take the maid to her doctor; she can give her groceries to take home to her children on her day off; she can give her her cast-off clothes; she can pay for the education of the maids' children; she can take the maid with her when she goes to Pampoenstad on vacation; and thousands of other good things like that: but she is doing for the maid what the maid would do for herself if she had the money.

"If the white woman were to buy heaven itself for the black woman in her employ, that would be hell. Nothing can make up for underpaying one's employee. Nothing, except increasing her wages.

"The dribs and drabs the white woman sees as charity are nothing but a salve to her conscience, an insult to the maid's dignity, and an assault to her self-esteem. The maid remains in a never-ending position of indebtedness. She works. Pay her and pay her justly. Then and only then does she become — even in the eyes of the medem — the adult she is.

"Feminism in this country has been retarded, in part, by this paternalistic attitude of white women towards black women. How can I be a sister to my father, the white woman?

"Living is learning. When is the domestic worker ever going to learn to mind her money if she never sees any? Two hundred rands. That's not enough for food money. Where is the rent for the four-room in Mdazzbhi? Children get sick. That's money for the clinic, money for medicine, and money for the special food doctors and nurses insist on when you take a child to them: 'Give her milk. Give her fruit. Give her fresh vegetable.' They don't tell you where you must get the money to buy all these things. Oh, no. And children's bodies are covered in bristle, from the way they tear away at clothes. Their clothes don't last at all. And the flimsy material the clothes-makers use don't help either. They make clothes that will not last; they make them that way so that you can come buying every other day. And then there is the money the schools demand. And the money the children demand to go to school — to buy *vetkoek* and cool drink.

The children want their school money otherwise they won't go to school. You who work for this money are the very last person to use any of it on yourself. Don't forget, the church wants its ticket money too. Mmmhh? No, the woman who works in the kitchen never has money. And this is a woman who is working, not part time but every day. She even sleeps at her place of work so, in a way, she works a twenty-four hour day, except for rest and sleep. With luck, she sees her own family less than ten waking hours a week. For two hundred lousy rands a month.

"Instead of being kind and buying this and that for the maid, just translate the kindness to this woman's wages — to rands and cents she can count on and knows are her due each month, whether or not your children have chicken pox or you need to replace your colored contact lenses or your husband's Mercedes must be serviced.

"Until white women do this, maids will remain stuck in poverty while in gainful employment. And I am sick and tired of people telling me about this one woman who bought a house for her maid. Who bought the house the maid cleans every day? The house the kind white woman lives in with her family? Do you hear her boss or her husband's boss going around crowing about how he bought a house for his employee? Why not?

"Because the boss probably doesn't even know whether his employee's house faces east or west, north or south. It is none of his business unless they are friends. Why do we become not just friends but family to the people we work for? People whose own families are bereft of kith?

"White people work. They earn. They live.

"We also work. We earn peanuts. We live in hope of living one day. But the one day never comes and we die poor, hoping still.

"Believe me, I mean it when I say I will not stay long in this kind of work. I would rather kill myself than be a nanny for the rest of my life. My mother is a domestic servant. So is her mother. And so was her mother and her mother before her. Four generations of domestic servants — that's enough. NO MORE. I refuse to be a slave.

"When I see myself cooped up in this box they call the maid's room I ask myself how the maids who have worked here didn't lose their minds. Imagine sleeping in a room whose walls look as if they could close in on you any minute you annoyed them. And then I think of all these women who work around here. Some are no longer young, you know? Why are they still here?

"Late at night, have you noticed all these men, fathers of children who are left to fend for themselves through the night, killing time near the shops waiting for the white families to go to sleep so they can come creeping to their wives and girlfriends?

"Mornings, see all the women in their uniforms taking white children to school. What a sight; until you ask yourself who takes the black child to school. And the white woman knows the black woman working for her has children. Knowing this, why is she not bothered by this mother in her house, the mother who never sees her children to school, who is never there when they return from school with some hurt, real or imagined, or when they have had a tough day just being children?

"These black women, in most cases, are more housekeepers than anything else. But no, in the eyes of the white women they work for they are children, worse than children: children grow up but domestic workers remain children to their death. When the white children the black woman raised become adults, they see the maid as a child, just as their parents have done all the time this woman has been working for them, smoothing their days and making them forget the coarser side of keeping house.

"White women may grow; they may become distinguished writers, champion golfers, renowned fashion designers, executives, and anything else; it is the unappreciated black women, who slave for them for next to nothing, who give them the time to indulge their fancies, follow their dreams, and live their fantasies to the fullest. 'Time is money,' don't we say? Then where is the money the black woman should get for her time?

"The time the white woman is given by the black woman who works for her, that time is more than money; it is freedom to the white woman: freedom to become whatever she would become. And she fails to see her indebtedness to the black maid who asks for so little in return: freedom from want, fair wage for sweat.

"These people I work for thought they were paying me a compliment: 'Read Penelope a story from her Xhosa book.' No mention of extra pay while I am being asked to tutor their daughter in Xhosa. Fine, it is my mother tongue and I am happy she is learning it; but can you imagine my mother asking the woman she works for to teach me English? The cheek. Of course, my poor mother wouldn't dream of such an imposition on her medem, but the medem thinks nothing of exploiting the maid. During my time, I must read a story so that their child's Xhosa can improve. And here I am, in the first place, when I would rather be in school. But that does not make them think of me as a student whose learning has been disturbed and who is pining for school. No. Even when they recognize that I can read, all they can think of is how that may benefit their child who deserves to be in school and to do well there. Me? I don't count except as a donkey that must work. I just told them I was not good at reading and I did not like stories. They haven't asked me again. I am waiting for the day they will ask me if I would like tutoring in, say English or Maths.

"I wonder what they will say when I tell them I'm taking Friday off next week. A meeting of students, teachers, and parents has been called for next Friday. I have to go. I want to be there when a decision is taken. I want to know what is going to happen so I can make appropriate plans. I am not going to see my twentieth birthday in this job. There is only one way for me to go from here: and, that is: OUT! . . . OUT! . . . OUT!"

8

Lillian

"My child, oh, if I was as young as you are, I would go back to school; go to night school. This slave work we do is no good. Look at me — gray hair, wrinkles, rheumatism — seven o'clock in the morning and I'm on my knees polishing the cold stoep outside. While my knees are creaking on the cement stoep — these children I work for are drinking their coffee in bed.

"Who do you think gave them that coffee in bed? Me. Old as I am. I have to get up, wash myself, before six o'clock. Six o'clock sharp — they want their coffee in bed. And they are not ashamed to take that coffee while they lie on their backs, warm in bed, from these gnarled hands. I'm old enough to be their grandmother. But then, white people don't respect age. To them, old is useless. That is all they see in me: old — useless.

"How long have I worked in the kitchens? How many years? And today I was told the brush doesn't do a good job: 'Lillian,' the woman said, 'you know the toilet bowl — down where the water goes out?

The brush can't go deep enough to get all the dirt. It can't get the corners.'

"Something told me she was giving me bad news. I waited for her to explain. I just knew she did not come to my room during my rest to tell me the brush is not long.

"'I want you to take a cloth and wash around the bowl. Use Vim, lots of Vim.'

"That is when I saw what she was saying. A cloth is worse than a brush. Does a cloth have any strength? Can a cloth rub harder than a brush? Is it longer?

"Do you know what this child wants me to do? Take my hand — MY HAND — and put it down there where their shit goes down. My hand must touch their shit. Not my shit; she wasn't talking about my toilet, mind you.

"Old as I am; I must take the shit of grown-ups in my hand. These people — when they pay you they think you are not a human being.

"What would she do if her own boss asked her to do something dirty like that, mmh? I wonder.

"Look at the room I sleep in. My tin *hokkie* in Crossroads is better. A chicken would suffocate in this thing, that is how small it is. But I am a servant; I am not supposed to have eyes to see when someone pushes me into a coffin and calls it a maid's room. Why didn't they put me in the garage? More room there — even with the two cars in it.

"One day, I wish whites would be forced to live like us. Just for one day. They would die like flies. And they would die screaming with the horrors — they'd be mad — mad — mad. Die of madness, they would. We really are strong — to live like we do.

"You know what she likes about me? She says, 'Lillian you really are good. I don't have to worry when I have people coming. You know what to do. Thank God you have experience.'

"But she doesn't think where this experience comes from. I bought it with my wrinkles, my aches and my pains. Age and long, hard work. That's what gave me the experience. And if she can see experience, she shouldn't be using it to polish stoeps at seven in the morning or to bring her coffee in bed at six. Experience should not take shit in its hand.

"All she worries about she says, when she has visitors, is whether I have enough to cook — enough of everything I will need. That is all she worries about.

"I worry about the dishes I'll have to wash. The smiles I'll have to fix on my face all the time. How many times I'll say 'Thank you, Medem. Thank you, Master' to all these people when they say something is nice or I'm a good cook. And all the time, all I want to do is put my old bones in bed. But I have to be smiling when they give me their stupid smiles that come from nowhere and mean nothing at all. I smile asking myself when did I become their friend or someone who won the July Handicap.

"Worked for her mother, I did. Brought her up since she was on her mother's breast. Now she gives her dog better meat than what she gives me. The money she spends on dog food, cat food, and the other things she needs for the animals — is more than she pays me. Are you telling me my price, in her eyes, is less than that of a dog?

"My own children and grandchildren don't eat things as good as those dogs and cats of hers eat: 'strue, I tell you. But I'm nailed here; I can't leave. When medem, that's her mother, when she left, she left my pension money with her daughter, this child, this thing I work for. That is my money and I'm going to wait for it even if I die; I'll die right here waiting for it. The mother went to live in England.

"All the years I worked hard for medem and master, this one's parents, when they paid me they always told me: 'Don't worry, Lillian my girl, when you're old you'll never need anything. We put money in the bank for you. Every time we pay you, we take a little from your money and add more; and that is what we're saving for, your old age.' Am I not old now?

"Oh, what did God do to me? Why did He have to take my master? That man! He was a good, kind man, a saint. I'm sure it was his idea that they put money in the bank for me. Medem . . . she was nice too. But stingy! It could never have been her idea to give me money for when I am old. No. Not her. She is nice but not kind. But, of course, why would God want her and not the kind one? Don't we say it is the beautiful dish that the gods will choose to take? Yes, they want the ones we value.

"Where is Imelda? Does she phone you? What! Never? You know, that Imelda is a funny child. Is she your age or older? Younger, I know she can't be. Go away, you think I will believe that?

"When are you finding yourself a young man . . . mmh? Let me warn you — I'm old enough to be your mother, my child: find a man if you don't want trouble from some of the masters around here; yours included, right in the front of the line too.

"That is how Imelda got into trouble. She would not say yes to any man. After some time she was staying in every night. Be careful of stay-in; especially if it's only the woman who is going out. Ask yourself why they need you to stay in if the father of the children is there. Ask yourself that or you will find yourself minding children who have beards. I don't trust Skinny Legs, your medem. I think she knows what her husband is up to with the black girls.

"But, why does she let her husband mess with the girls? I'm sure she knows but I can't see why she lets it happen; why she pretends she doesn't see it.

"Poor Imelda. I didn't like her very much. But I must say I felt very much pained for her. Yes, my heart ached for her. Especially after that business of hers; she nearly died; did you hear about that?

"That happened a year or so after she came to work for the no-legs woman. Still pretending she didn't have hot blood like everybody else. No, to the milkman. No, to the gardener. No, to the man who works at the flower shop. And no, to Sophie's husband, a clerk at the Bantu Administration Office. Don't give me those eyes. Men will always be dogs; they will have more than one woman, my child. It has been like that since the time of our forefathers.

"Well, my child, I wasn't born yesterday. Imelda must have said yes to somebody. I saw her back grow and spread sideways and become stiff; making itself strong to carry the heaviness.

"But me, I'm not forward. I wait until things come to me. I wait and open my eyes. I wait and, AHA! Doesn't she start wearing overalls day in and day out? Even when she's off duty?

"Then her eyes get white, very white. That's always a sign. The white of the eyes, they become white like a baby's.

"You know? Your people — that woman knows, *suuka!* I'm not a child. They send her to their doctor. End of story, my child. The woman is so flat you can think someone ironed her stomach for her. Flat. Flat. Flat . . . like a bug in a long-deserted house.

"But she nearly died. And that was the last time her eyes got white like that. Poor Imelda.

"Then she was getting married. And then she not getting married. Then, she was saying yes to all the men. She was sleeping with half the men around here. One wife came all the way from the location — she came here and made quite a row over there where you work. The policc had to be called.

"Even today, I hear Imelda still sleeps with anything that wears pants.

"You, get yourself a young man, I am warning you. If the husband of this strange woman you work for doesn't soon hear a man's cough here some nights . . . you will become his business; of that I can assure you. Don't say I didn't tell you, one day. It's long ago that I first saw the sun, I tell you.

"My daughter once had a master like the one you've got. She was afraid even of being in one room with him. And men like him, white men like that, they will always find an excuse to talk to the girl. There they have a wife who should be telling the girl what's what, but, no. They must be the ones who tell her. Sometimes, they will even go to the girl's room, any time — day or night. Then you know they are not good. What do they want with a girl? Isn't it the medem who should be worrying about the maid?

"But when my daughter was working for a woman with such a husband, she was herself already a woman. She had been with a husband of sorts; you know the kind that has never heard of *lobola?* The African who wants to think he is a colored and just takes a wife? My daughter's husband was that kind. A dog. My poor child had to work hard, char jobs for a long time. This husband of hers did not know that children eat. So she was no spring chicken and knew how to look after herself.

"I trained my daughter. There is nothing she cannot do: she bakes cakes even. When medem, the mother of this one, the one who went to England, when she was having visitors for the summer (you know how the rough necks from Pretoria come flocking here to our beaches) she would ask me to ask my daughter to come and help out. That kept her out of mischief during the six weeks school vacation. She worked there right alongside me. And she was given a good sum too.

"By the time she was fifteen and I took her out of school she could clean, cook, do the laundry, baby-sit — everything. Medem gave her good references and she got a job easily. Her second job was the one she is still doing today. She will die with these people, I think. She works at the home of the French Ambassador. And those whites from overseas do not have this apartheid. They pay her much more than anybody I know; anybody working in kitchen work, that is.

"If this woman-with-no-legs you work for tries to mess you up, remember, my daughter has connections in all the embassies. She even got her daughter, the eldest one, a job with another one, the American Embassy. Her daughter isn't even working in the kitchen. A girl who only has JC, and she makes tea at the office of these Embassy people. What do you think of that?

"We work for nothing in these kitchens. You would faint if I told you how much my granddaughter, the one who makes tea for the Embassy people, if I told you how much money they give her. That child makes more money a week that I make in a whole month. And, friend, she has a pension. A pension that she can see on her envelope. Yes, her wages comes in an envelope, signed with her name. Nobody calls her when she feels like it and says in a voice that has no warmth, 'Here, Lillian.' And then asks you: 'Are you happy?' as if she has just given you something for nothing. As if you did not work, sweat, for what she was giving you. And all you can do is paste a smile on your face and say: 'Of course, yes, medem, I'm very happy, medem.' Mmhh?

"Have you noticed how these women suddenly lose their nice smiles when it is time to pay us? You can see her mind working overtime: Why am I giving my money to this Bantu woman? She has forgotten your sweat, your knees, your wrists that are forever chafed from doing her laundry by hand; your blistered hands that are too familiar with the iron are nothing to her; she grieves for the rands she is forced to give to you. That is why some of them will find any excuse to take away some of that money that they should be giving to you. End of the month, you hear all sorts of excuses from the white women: 'This and that is missing. I see you chipped this plate. What did you do with master's blue tie?' Then, you must know; she wants to help herself to your wages. These are not people we work for.

"Me? My child I am not lying to you; if I were your age I would go to night school. I would learn and become something. Kitchen work is just the work of slaves. We live to work, that's all. Nothing else. It is no life. No life at all."

9

Atini's reflections

So I went to East London, although I did not have a pass to work there. I knew there were many women in the same stew; in the cities, working and risking arrest for being there without permission. Well, if they stayed in the village they risked death. People die from not having food to eat, you know. There was nothing for me to do but follow that example. East London is the nearest big town to Gungululu, the village where my husband's people live.

No one knew I was leaving. Even I did not know, for although I had thought and thought about it, about going to work, I did not know when or how or where to start. Until the night I knew, with absolute certainty, that that was all I could do. The only thing I could do to be a mother. If I had not done that, I know that today not one of my children would still be living. And, perhaps, neither would I. We would all be dead. Of hunger.

I know not to read. I cannot write. And I did not have a pass. Those are very big stumbling blocks in anybody's way. More so to a mother of five children who has a mother-in-law who never once said "no" to her only son, her only child.

Me, my child, believe me, I have lived. I have lived and life has been no mattress made of chicken feathers. Far from it. But now, the hardship I carry on my shoulders is a different hardship. Every day I put food into my mouth. Every month I send money to my children in the village. The bigger three are still there, only the youngest two are here with me. They live with a woman who looks after babies and young children in her house in Mdantsane. Whenever I'm off, I go to see them there. Of course, I pay the woman for her trouble. I am not saying I pay her enough; but where would I get the money to pay anyone enough? I don't get enough myself. Enough is not for people like me. It is a word that has one meaning for us. Trouble. That is about the only thing we have enough of. Not wages. Not food. Not money. Not clothes. Not children's books. Not house. Not marriage. Not doctors. No. Enough is trouble for us. Any way you look at it. With the money I get at the end of the month, how could I pay anyone enough? But I take a little and pay her and send a little to the village where my poor children are. It is not much that I send there, but then, we are not used to much in our lives. I am grateful we are alive. It's been two years and eight months since that long-ago night I left my home and my children in their sleep. That means I have been working for Kindling-Legs for two years and six months. In all that time, I have been back to the village only once. That's when I brought Sizwe and the baby, Thandiwe, to East London. I hadn't seen my children for all of twelve months before I made that trip.

Nomakhwezi is the woman of that home. She cooks for her brother, Andile, and her sister, Nomso. She also teaches them work. I was very happy to see how they really look after themselves although Manala, my mother-in-law, does see to things. Not a day since I left, the children tell me, has she not shown her face at my home. So, maybe it was the right thing to do, for her, I mean. When would she have known those are her grandchildren? She was so careful not to come anywhere near me. But now, I can't complain. She is good to the children and we have become closer than I would ever have believed.

Their father too has been back. The first time he returned to find me gone he put on his longest face and went to the village of my own family. There, my people laughed at him as if his pants had dropped to his ankles, in full view of the whole village. "You left here, years ago, with our daughter," they said. "Today, after she has given you so many children, when you have a misunderstanding, you come to us? Had she been a bad wife, we believe we would have seen your face here within weeks of your taking her. You, it is, who must be a bad husband."

That is what my people told my husband. They say he left like a dog who returns from a hunt with a fox bite. Unfortunately, when I went back I missed him by a few days. Perhaps it was just as well. What would he have said to me? And I to him? He had been there a whole month and had been gone less than a week when I arrived. I wish I could tell him a thing or two . . . but since we are "red" and cannot write, how can I? But, never mind, I'm sure he must know why I did what I did. Unless he is a bigger fool than I think he is.

And here in the city, are all these women wearing the same blanket or do my eyes fail to see the different pattern? Are they all enveloped in sorrow? Or is the plaintive, melancholy note I hear only an echo of what sounds in my own heart?

The young woman, so sure she is here not for long when I first met her, is still here. Time, for us, crawls with the slow step of a chameleon returning from a feast. She says she is applying to training hospitals to go and learn to be a nurse: a stop-gap measure, she says, a detour on her way to becoming doctor. I, myself, wish her luck, I pray she succeeds. But I know a lot of the other maids laugh at her behind her back. They do not believe she will escape from this place. They say she can forget about education. And they may be right. Since her mother died, who will pay for that now?

She is only four years older than Nomakhwezi and perhaps that is why I want to believe in her dreams. I have dreams too for my children although I don't tell them to the others. Dreams are like secret lovers; elusive and prone to bolt if you divulge them. I lock mine up in the deepest chamber of my heart and only take them out on lonesome nights. And then, like a magic mirror, they dazzle me with bounteous hope for the morrow.

The old woman's hopes of a pension are also still on hold. As luck would have it, the young woman she was working for, the woman she raised when she worked for the medem who went to live in England, that poor woman died: car accident. A drunken driver ploughed into her car. And, although the other driver was in the wrong, God chose to take the woman. There just is no fairness in life, I guess.

Well, the other unfair thing is that in her will she did not say anything about the maid. Now this poor soul, the old woman, is waiting until her master has had time to mourn and then she will bring up this problem. She wants him to write to his mother-in-law, her former medem, to find out about her pension. Meanwhile, she says she is old enough to get *nkam-nkam*, that is the pension from the government; but she is afraid to apply for it: everyone who gets it has told her it is nothing but chicken feed. Also, everyone knows that as soon as a person gets *nkam-nkam*, that person will soon die. It seems to be bad luck. So she wants to go on working although she does not know whether her master will want her to stay on or what. Terrible, if he didn't want her. With her creaking knees, think any white woman'll give her a job? He hasn't told her anything about his plans now that he is a widower. So she waits; and hopes. We carry hope the way sailors do lifejackets. Without it I sometimes think we would all be in Fort Beaufort, you know? Where they lock up people whose minds have left them.

Not a few of the maids I found here when I first came have lost their jobs and gone to work in other areas. One left with the white people she worked for and two or three were left here when their medems, including the Advice Office woman who was always telling us about our rights, went overseas with their families. Those took even their cats and dogs with them but not one of them even talked about taking their maid. Which proves it doesn't matter how long a maid stays with these people and how many times a day they tell her: "Oh, Sheila, we love you and we don't know what we'd do without you," — when they decide what to do about themselves, it is their cars, their dogs, their cats, their houses, their friends and their anything-else-but-the-maid they think about. And pity the maid they do think about: she will be left with all their broken furniture, whatever they cannot take with them because the children grew up climbing on it and the cats have scratched all the paint from it. She will have to paint the biggest lie of a smile on her face as she thanks them for rags she will herself throw away.

But I'm not saying medems have it good all the time. They also have their problems; I mean, with maids. Take poor Mrs. Reed for example.

From the first day with Mrs. Reed I was struck by her helplessness. For this woman, the maid is not just someone else who is there to work for her, no. Mrs. Reed's girl soon gets to know that she is this medem's extension: her arms, her legs, and her eyes. The only active part of the body this woman has is the mouth. And she uses it every hour of the day to tell you: "Do this. Do that."

I left my baby and came to this town to work. What do I find? Here I am working for another baby, a grown-up baby called Mrs. Reed. The woman is really, really useless. I am surprised she can wash herself in the bath; wash and dry herself and put on her own clothes.

Other medems stretch their legs. Not her: "Go to the flower shop and get me a bunch of gladioli or marigolds if they don't have gladioli." That's another thing about white women: they hate to see anything free. The flowers of the veld — made for fresh air, sunshine, and freedom — they pluck and imprison inside their houses. Like us, the flowers have no choice.

Sticks can use the phone to order meat from the butchery: but why not send the maid? It's cheaper. Now I know all the cuts of meat you can get: cutlets, chops, steak, and God knows what else. All because she saves her money and won't phone her orders through as the other medems do. I get her meat for her. I take her shoes to the shoemaker and her clothes to the cleaners. When her son's birthday is coming I go to CNA to get a card for her: "Get a nice one," she says. And while she is busy sitting in front of her TV, I must take my tired legs that have been all over her house cleaning to CNA and she knows I cannot read. "Ask the medems who work there to help you." That's how she helps me. This woman is too lazy even to write a note and explain what she wants. Me, with my broken English, I must go and find a nice birthday card for her son.

But the white women aren't having a good time all the way. With having maids, it can't be that much fun to have to take a total stranger into your home. Not all maids are good people. I've seen not a few I wouldn't want myself in my home. But because the white woman tells herself and believes she needs a maid she will take anything that comes to her door when she is desperate.

And I'm sure there is some truth in some of the stories I hear: maids stealing or helping burglars break into the homes where they work; maids wearing the medem's choice dresses on the sly; maids helping themselves to their masters (naturally, with the encouragement of these masters). Of course, that doesn't say all maids do such things. But I can see the problem of the white woman opening her home to a black woman and trusting her completely — with children, with everything in the home, and with one's very life . . . in illness and accidents, for example. No wonder most medems walk around with deep worry furrows on their faces.

One bad experience with a maid, and all the bad things a medem has heard about maids are confirmed. From then on, the maid in her employ will feel her scorching eyes dogging her throughout each day in whatever she does: "How many shirts were in the wash?" the medem asks, counting the shirts just ironed. That's the worst thing for a maid — to be under such constant suspicion when she herself has done nothing to deserve it. It is this that reminds her that, to her medem, she is not a person in her own right but one of a group; and not a good group at that.

Why can't the medem deal with each maid as a separate person? Why can't she treat her right until the maid shows herself as undeserving of such treatment? Wouldn't it be better to show a new maid trust? Might she not then respond by proving worthy of that trust? Why would a woman not steal when she knows she is expected to anyway?

Yes, the white women chain themselves to black women by believing themselves so helpless. Or by so valuing soft hands, chatting on the phone, going to the beautician, and all the things having free time gives them, that they have come to need black women so much. Their need of us in their homes beats their dislike and suspicion of us. They are slaves to the leisure and luxury that having servants gives them. Yes, they are slaves just as we are slaves. We need each other . . . we need each other to survive.

The day I stole away from my children I was so sad that if I had not had those children to get money for I'd have killed myself. They are the only reason I'm still here, the one reason I will go on doing this job that is killing me. At least it is giving life to them. For my children I will go on being killed every day, slowly but surely, by kitchen jobs. How can I leave them?

Therefore, all of us maids say the same thing: we work for nothing but it is better than not working and dying in one day or one week. We work and send our children to school and hope we will not die before we've seen them grown.

Meanwhile, we laugh a lot about our work in the kitchens of white women. We laugh because if we did not laugh what would we do? Cry? Which maid would help which other one wipe away the tears?

No longer will I ask: What is hell? I know it because I am there. I know it because all these women tell me they are there. Yes, the words are different — some are angry words and others are sad and sorry words. I have even heard a few words of praise. But, deep down, all the words tell the same story. We are slaves in the white women's kitchens.

That is how I see it. I ran away from that hell of starvation, torn clothes, sick children. And I came here to work so that I would feed my children, clothe them, send them to school, and have money to take them to the doctor if they are seriously ill. Now, I find that I am in hell. And I am a slave.

These children I work for, I do not see. Soon I will be a stranger to them. The money I earn will never do even half of those things I came here to work for.

But I am not alone. All the other women, like me, are suffering. That is why we laugh about our troubles. That is why. We have so many and they are the same — it is like a nightmare that gives us no rest. It is with us by night and by day. So, we laugh about it.

But when a woman is alone — alone at night and can't sleep thinking of all these problems — then, she cries. She cries because she can see she may never escape from this hell.

There's some good news I've just heard.

Aren't the ways of the Man Upstairs strange? Aren't they wonderful? Joyce has told me she has a scholarship. She is going to a school overseas and if she does well they will help her to study to become a doctor. Oh, I am so happy for her. Shows you . . . you have to be determined. There *are* ways. If you know what you want and you don't give up . . .

PART TWO

. . . And other stories

10

Flight

Cries of "*Khawulele! Wenk'umntu!*" shattered the stillness of the saucer-like village nestling in the valley, surrounded by green hills and scrub-dotted mountains.

Echoes bounced from hilltops, clashed mid-air, ricocheted and fell in jumbled noises that boomed, invading our ears and jamming out all other sounds.

weh weh weh khauu khauu khauu
leh leh leh leh tuu tuu tuu!

Like a powerful magnet, the commotion pulled us away from the rag dolls that had so occupied us but a moment before.

Iii-ii-iiiii Wuu-uuuuu!
Mmbaaa — mbeeehh-ni!
Qhaaa-wuu-leee-laani!

An old man, short, tight-curled springs of wool on his head making a grayish-white skull cap, tottered past in what I saw was his earnest attempt at running. His left hand clasped the blanket loosely wrapped around his body; his right arm, from the shoulder, was stuck out as if from a toga. Thin, long, and bony, it swung back and front in time to his intended accelerated step. Held high in the hand, a knobkerrie jutted out and away from his body. Each time he shouted "*Mbambeni!* — Catch her!" he stretched out the arm holding the knobkerrie, pointing the stick towards the mountain.

My eyes leapt to where he pointed. The mountain was playing a game of hide and seek with the sun. Or was it with the clouds? Anyway, half the mountain had disappeared. I threw my eyes towards the remaining half. There, distance-shrunk figures scurried, hurried, ran, and scrambled.

Ahead, a long figure darted like a hare with a pack of dogs hard on its tail. The clouds were no idle players, I saw. They were the third party to this game; and they would make the telling difference.

Clearly, that day, I witnessed the birth of tears. The clouds wept and showered soft tears of mist onto the silent mountain. Would the fleeing figure gain the mist blanket in time? The sun smiled and the mist disappeared in a spray of long, hot, yellow needles, the children of the sun.

There she was, clearly, I saw her. Surely, her pursuers too could see her? — see her as I did?

My insides churned. A hot ball of fear curled inside my stomach. But the clouds, not to be outdone, wept. Thick, fat, dark gray spears fell. Fast and hard they came. Thick, fat; safe for her to be enveloped in and lost to her pursuers.

"*Uye phi? Uye phi?* Where's she gone?"

Sounds of distress from those who were bent on her capture reached me. I held my breath as I strained with her, willing her to elude them, urging her on and on and on.

My last glimpse of her: blue German-print dress paled to a soft sky-blue by distance and lack of light . . . there she was, flitting here and there between boulders, her long new-wife-length dress making her seem without feet. As she hurried, escaping, she appeared to me to be riding the air — no part of her body making contact with the ground.

Away she floated; the men plodded behind her.

I saw her waft into the wall of mist. I saw it close the crack she'd almost made gliding into it. Like a fish slicing into water, she'd but disturbed it. And it rearranged itself, accepting her into itself. And away from those who harried her.

I cannot remember her face at all. It was a long time ago and perhaps she had not tarried long with us. I don't know. But I remember her leaving. And that is because it taught me about determination, the power of one's will.

She was a young woman, a new wife. Her husband, my uncle, was away at work in one of the mines where all the men of the village went for a very long time. Later, much later, with great learning to aid me order my world, I would come to know the precise length of their stay — eleven months each year. However, this knowledge was light years away from me that fear-filled day long, long ago.

It must have been midday, for the sun was well up and we children were already outside at play; that is, those of us too little to go to the one mud-walled, grass-thatched house called school.

I know I should've been sad at losing an aunt. I know she was a good *makoti*, cooked and cleaned well, and we children were saved from a lot of chores by her coming — new wives are worked like donkeys as initiation into their new status. I know I should have sympathized with my uncle who lost not only a wife but also the cattle, the *lobola*, he had given for her.

All I know, is the thrill I felt watching her escape into the thick gray cloud and mist.

11

The most exciting day of the week

Monday, school. Tuesday, school. Wednesday, school again. More school Thursday; and more on Friday. But Friday was different.

Friday was a day on which things happened. When I was a child, everything but everything happened on Friday. There were exceptions, of course: logical. Burials were on Saturdays, weddings on Sundays, witchdoctors' dances on either of those. But Friday bustled. It was a busy day, a noise-filled, sweaty, smelly day that stretched long, fun-filled, and generous. It began before the alarm of other school mornings rang and went on and on and on, well past the usual sleeptime. There was none of the same deadness of other days on Friday, a jewel of a day.

Long, pungent fingers are forcing themselves down nostrils; have crept deep into the head and switched eyes on. Awake, I lie in bed and slowly inhale; drinking in the acrid, musty smell of fermented kaffircorn sprouts (*inkoduso*).

Eyes gain focus, gradually. Two big drums stand tear-stained against the opposite wall. Down their old, rusty cheeks run fawn zig-zags, some dark, almost the same color as the rust of the drums — tell-tale marks of the secret within. Beer that has gurgled and bubbled all night through and, full of its own glee, has tumbled over the rims and cascaded down the cheeks in foamy somersaults; crusting here, running forever there — to go on and dry just the same: little wiggledy piggledy columns of fawn crust of uneven thickness and length.

Soft, ever so soft, hushed sibilant whisperings come to me as I lie still: very, very still. "Hshhhsssshhss ssshshshhsssh hhsssshshshsh," the beer is impatient to complete its journey; do what it was meant to do. I imagine it pleading — "Please let me be. Please let me be"— in its language, of course. And my heart goes out to it for that is exactly what I would like to say to Mother, who is nowhere in sight. Her presence though, is always with me. Even now, the very thought of her breaks the line of communication with the beer; for unless one concentrates and is completely quiet, beer talk is wholly inaudible. Ears strain, but the spell is broken. Silence is my only reward. Then I hear the door creak open.

Mother bounds into focus. She is carrying two four-gallon cans, shiny as new silver coins. She puts them clangingly next to the drums. The gaping mouth of one she caps with a metal strainer shaped like a basin. A round strainer in a four-cornered mouth. Yet it fits, sort of.

Sleeves rolled up, Mother picks up the two-pint metal scoop lying near the drums on old newspapers. This she puts on top of the sieve and takes a longish, thin plank standing between the two drums and leaning against the wall. She uncovers one of the drums, puts the plank in and begins to stir. The flat pivot and Mother's plump arms form a tripod.

In a raised voice, the beer protests. Gone is the shy whispering. Hoarse, harsh whooshes and whhishhes come from the drum as Mother continues to stir. The beer is thick: mealie-meal, kaffircorn sprouts and yeast are but some of the ingredients. Round and round goes the plank to Mother's gyrating body, her arms drawing circles in the air above the whooshing drum.

Out comes the plank. Mother wipes it by scraping it along the drum's rim: first this side and then the other. Now she puts it to rest, once more, against the wall, wet side up.

Bent over the strainer-covered can, Mother takes the scoop and dips it into the drum she has just stirred. Out it comes, all heavy and dripping from the beer in its belly and that coating it outside. Mother empties the scoop onto the strainer.

Immediately, rat-a-tat little punches tap the bottom of the can as the liquid jets through the small, round peepholes of the strainer. Again Mother scoops more unstrained beer into the sieve. Three or four times, and the strainer is full.

Lethargically, the beer drains through the sieve. To encourage it, Mother's hand worries, moving side to side in the thick unstrained beer, clearing the pores of the sieve. The sound changes. Now it is thick and full; fast like a sudden summer shower sloshing onto sandy puddles.

Mother's left hand holds the sieve faithfully glued to the can's mouth. It is her right hand, however, that holds my eyes spellbound. Like the eager tail of a spaniel welcoming the family back from a long vacation, it wags furiously deep into the strainer. But I do not see the hand; totally gloved by the beer. Thus her arm appears chopped off at the wrist. However, I am not alarmed for I know the amputation is but illusory. As needed, the hand comes up from beneath the dense, foaming liquid.

Again and again, she fills the thirsty strainer from the drum; and helps push the beer through into the can. And as the chaff accumulates in the strainer, she empties it into a basin standing nearby for exactly that very purpose. Her hand dips deeper and deeper into the drum as the now almost silent can gives only the satisfied lush sounds of a replete stomach. It is full.

It is time to start on the second can. But, instead, Mother remembers other chores. Few customers come for a drink this early and the one can should suffice for now.

"While you're busy throwing big eyes at me," says Mother, not looking at me directly, "time isn't waiting for you." The voice, a whip, reminds me of what the teacher will do to me if I am late for school. No second bidding is necessary.

I scramble out of bed. In a tin mug, coffee is cooling next to a *vetkoek* on a saucer. Although I'm famished I but glance their way as I make mine outside. Right next to the door, a basin waits; standing guard over a crookedly rectangular piece of blue soap. Cut from a long bar, its edges are uneven; it smiles a partly toothless-child lopsided smile.

I stoop and hastily wash hands, arms, face, and legs. Then back into the house I bolt. The coffee is lukewarm by now. That is the only way I drink it. I am never ready simultaneously with Mother's plonking the mug on the table. Least of all on Friday.

I scurry into my school uniform with bulging mouth. I've long mastered the art of doing several things all at once. No one said everything has to be done perfectly. I'm only certain I will not be naked as I run to school.

Beer bottles and stout bottles stand in dignified assemblage at the far corner: a forest of dark brown, almost black shapes, sturdy trunked and long necked; empty. They wait for the mail, the man who buys liquor for Mother. Illegally. Even as I mumble, "I'm off," that lady is wide-eyed, ordering a mound of coins into sense-making columns: forty twenty-cent pieces and ten five-cent pieces are ten bottles of Old Buck Dry Gin, a case of Lion Lager comes from twenty ten-cent pieces and fifteen five-cent pieces and five twenty-cent pieces. I exit to the tinkling of little coins.

My route to school, even on Fridays, is strangely without memories. School is school: dull and dreadful. Teachers would have deprived me of the bliss of Friday. However, they could never penetrate that inner place, the place of knowing and understanding. The place where joy and all thoughts of gladness dwell. In that place, firmly stamped, was the knowledge of the afternoon's promise. After school, life would begin. Begin in earnest. That I knew and no teacher could rob me of that blissful knowing. FUN was out there waiting. Only the last school bell stood between me and a whole long stretch of joy.

School dismissal was special agony on Fridays: long and tedious. The prayers invariably included a request to the Almighty to "watch over these innocent little lambs throughout the weekend." And some of the little lambs sorely needed all the protection they could get. Friday was settle scores day. Weeklong quarrels, resentments and slights, gossip and slander, suspicion of theft, and anything else, all these were settled on Fridays — after school. This was the convention. It was that way when I started school. It was that way when I left. I believe it is still so today.

On Friday, as the multitude shoves, jostles, and hurls itself out of the narrow school gate, little clumps form. Not so near the school as to attract a teacher's eye, though.

Both the accused and the aggrieved have supporters. These "friends" guarantee the fight will take place. By Friday it is too late to permit a cancelation. The crowd already smells blood; and nothing short of blood will appease it.

With faces turned to fiercesome masks of hatred, the fighters face each other, their skirts hitched up and tucked into the elastic of the bloomers' legs. Responding to the boisterous encouragement of their respective camps, they fall on each other like dogs over a bone.

The drunken, heaving wrestling is punctuated with errant punches that exhaust the puncher more than they harm the target. The luckier of the two trips the other and falls on top of her. But instead of punching the daylights out of her, now is the time she will vent all her venom: "Didn't I tell you I would get you? Can you repeat what you said to so-and-so about me? Who did you call what?"

The antics held my fascination: bared thighs, and bloomers that often wore holes the size of potatoes; tears that escaped despite valiant attempts at keeping them from spilling; and the feverish thrill of the crowd, itself safe from any humiliation.

Fights usually ended when one of the fighters took off or an adult happened on the scene. In the latter case, we all ran for dear life, afraid of being associated with such a misdeed should it be reported to the teachers.

As in my memory I near home, Friday location scenes hit me, blotting away the everyday shabbiness — the sand I walk, dirty to almost black and filled with debris of every imaginable kind, today is a welcome carpet. How could it matter that we had no streets or roads, tarred or otherwise; wasn't that the fisherman's horn?

"Mmpmmpooh-mpppmmpooh! Mppmmmpoohh-mmppmpooh!" Two short blasts, pause, two short blasts; the sound comes from far west of my home. I pray the horse-drawn cart has already been to us and that Mother has bought some fish.

Outside our door. Smell assaults senses. Smell irrigates mouth to wetness. It hangs my eyes on stalks, rotates my neck a full 360 degrees. Fish. Samp. Not the boiled-to-death, tasteless mess of other days, samp cooked with meaty bones, potatoes, onion, and tomatoes, seasoned with heady spices: bouillon cube, mixed masala, pepper, and a whole bar of Pret.

Indeed, the whole house is transformed. The floor has been scrubbed; the planks bleached the khaki of old bones. I imagine Mother kneeling on the floor, skirt girded high, to just above the knees, scrubbing-brush toing and froing on the wet plank floor. Occasionally, she fishes out the old vest we use as a mop, wrings it dry, and wipes the sudsy, scummy water off the floor.

Mother's hands would still be wrinkled. The harsh soap, the blue all-purpose soap we use, does that to one's hands after a time. And I know it takes a long time to scrub the entire floor. The acrid scent of the soap lingers still, a sign of an earnest cleanup. As I walk into the house, my feet print themselves onto the floor's pale face.

Inside, the spotless house is pervaded by the heavy scent of Indian incense sticks. Well hidden from view, their scent does not mingle with any of the other smells but rises above them; cementing our belief that the sticks were good luck and burning them pulled customers into the house.

Intricately patterned newspaper hangs on cupboard and on table. Eva, the colored cleaning-woman, was here. This I know for Mother does not know how to cut out those lacy patterns on newspapers. Only colored women and those African women who've been long in the towns know how to do that. Everywhere, the house is one big sparkle.

But, of all the transformation that Friday brought, none was more spectacular than that wrought on Mother. Long, married-woman skirt, slightly hitched up, revealed yellow legs glistening with glycerine or Vaseline or other oil. Instead of the German print frock she wore every day, on Fridays Mother wore *isishweshwe*, gaily bordered along the hemline with rows and rows of colorful braid which we called kalamazoo. I understood that looking attractive was part of her business arsenal. Her customers were almost all men and were more likely to support her if she looked attractive. Well, she wore a shine in her eye the way flowers open petals to bees and, up close, there was the slightest whiff of lavender.

Father was the only man I knew who did not drink on Friday. He had to stay sober, he said, so that if any of Mother's customers got out of hand he would be able to help.

"Ma-athaa-a-ammboo-o! Maa-athaa-a-ammbboo-o!"

"Been en bottel! Been en bottel!"

That was another welcome Friday sound; a bounteous one too. This one actually promised us money. As the ragman called out, we went hurrying and scurrying, searching for bones we had safely buried only to find them gone; dogs and other similarly motivated little persons having discovered our loot. Hastily, we gather whatever we can lay our hands on and take it to the ragman's cart. At a shilling a can, none of us children could afford to disregard this gentleman's call. And, served with neither trash cans in our homes nor refuse collection in the township, the wide expanse of sand on which the shacks we called homes were haphazardly strewn was, indeed, a veritable mine. Bones we found galore and only time stood in our path to wealth.

Heavenly noises added to the magic of Friday, shrinking the distance between dream and reality. Either we did not notice that much air traffic on other days, or it just wasn't there for us to notice. I don't know which is true. However, on Friday afternoons, late afternoons, planes would come flying low over the location where we lived. This was so especially in the summer, if my memory is correct. I recall our excited cries, always in the singular although this was a group activity:

"Eropleyni! 'zundiphathel'ibanana! 'zundiphathel'iapile! 'zundiphathel' ilokhwe!" (Aeroplane, bring me a banana. Bring me an apple. Bring me a dress.) As part of the long, lazy, sun-drenched days of summer. The cries are accompanied by frantic waves as we make sure the fliers see us, see what we look like, who we are. We waved to the pale, barely discernible pink blobs. They waved back. Magic waved back at us! Why would we not have been carried away and ask for things we did not ask for from our parents? New dresses, bananas, sweets, dolls. Could anything be beyond such people who could fly? Not to us. So we made our requests; unhindered by reality. They were just part of the marvel of Friday, those people who could fly.

The throaty sounding of *umgqala kaMashushu*, as we called the siren of the only industrial concern near enough to our location for the men who worked there to go to work on foot, announced FIVE

O'CLOCK. *Mashushu* was officially known as THE METAL BOX COMPANY and, at the sounding of its siren, out would flock hundreds and hundreds of men. These were the forerunners of the influx of our fathers, grandfathers, uncles, and older brothers. If the men from *Mashushu* had come, could the men from the farms and the firms and the dock be far behind? That siren, in a place where no one had wrist watches and few homes boasted an alarm clock, was our unfailing aural clock.

First to come, of course, would be Mother's customers from *Mashushu*. But soon thereafter the others would come. This was busy time.

Even before I had started school, I had learnt to help Mother make her sales. A nip, half a bottle, or a bottle from a gallon, I could measure by age five. By six I could pour out a beaker of kaffir beer. And by seven I could not only be sent to the shop but could be relied on to bring back the correct amount of change.

Night. This was the best time of the best of days. Unlike other days when homework and parental concern nailed one down to the house, Friday night was carefree night. Often, one of the men would bring a guitar or harp or mouth organ and music would fill the night; making fantastic an already magical day.

Also, the people drinking beer and liquor would want something from the shop. Guess who would be sent there? From sundown to well past bedtime, I became part of the drunken delight of the location's Friday Night.

Babu, the Indian shopkeeper, kept a switch visible on the counter on Fridays. The shop was always crowded on Fridays and some people took that as a sign they could help themselves to what they wanted since Babu was doing so well. Except that Babu did not share this opinion. And was not above using the switch on a child he caught stealing or about to steal.

Going to the shop was always fun. Going there at night was a real treat that I only got on Friday when too many people wanted too many things at different times. Then, even I got to have a chance to go to the shop at night. Although all the adults who sent us to the shop were bound to give us some spending money, a child was truly lucky to be sent to the shop by an adult who had already had too much to drink. A drunk hand is a more open hand, this I discovered in my childhood Fridays. Not only would such a person give me a lot more money than I expected, he would give me more than he suspected; often more than he spent on whatever he had wanted from the shop. Moreover, having forgotten how much he had given one in the first place, he just as easily might say "Keep the change" upon receiving his purchase. Of course, with the uncanny insight of childhood, I soon recognized my true beneficiaries, men who'd had too much with their first drink. I tried to get these same men to send me to the shop on Fridays. They were my regulars.

All the shops were on the Main Road, a good distance from our township. To get there, one had to leave the township, walk through a wooded area, past avenues of houses where colored people lived, and then, there was the Main Road all a-glitter: electric street lamps, shop lights and neon lights, cars zooming up and down the street, buses even.

However, more than the glitz of our mini-city pulled us outdoors and to the Main Road on these nights. The camaraderie of our mates, the money in our hands, what we bought with it, the license to be abroad late at night, all these together did not have the magnetic pull of another pursuit, one clandestine and verging on the dangerous: following, at great and discreet distance, lovers too absorbed in each other as they sought a "safe" spot in the woods. Once this poor, unsuspecting couple settled down, their secret was whispered, like a password, to each child or group of children one passed on the way.

Not that we were much enlightened by our spying. The thrill lay in just watching something we all knew we were not supposed to watch, some adult secret. Of course, we faced beatings if caught. And we never revealed this fringe benefit of Friday night shopping to our unsuspecting parents. And, although this had the breath-holding excitement of fear of discovery, we wearied soon of watching something that did not seem to amount to anything. Then we contented ourselves with passing the word on to others while we went on to more satisfying activities.

Money from the ragman, money from Mother's customers who felt benevolent for no reason at all except its being Friday, money from those of them who had sent me to the shop: didn't we splurge on Fridays!

Cream doughnuts, milk chocolate, fish and chips, fish crumbs, Stars and Sharpe toffees, Menth-o-lyptus, all these, depending on how much I'd made, would waltz down my throat, their slippery sweetness a thrill to remember . . . until next Friday.

Well into the night, we were up and busy helping Mother in her business. This was a chance for me to stay up as late as late can be. Even as sleep would thwart my ambitions, I would fight it off as long as I possibly could. And sometimes disturbances would help me stay up later than I could have thought possible: fights between two men or groups of men, wife-beatings, police raids.

And from the vantage point of a child, I came to associate Friday and all it stood for with one thing: money. Money was the one ingredient not present on any other day, only Friday. Friday was payday.

Therefore, long before I reached Standard Three and learnt clever phrases and idioms, I knew that money made the world go round. However, I knew also that it was the root of all evil. And I knew that Friday was the day on which its spirit breathed itself into the people of the African location where I lived; who, thus transfigured, walked and talked and laughed and smiled, played and ate and sang and jived. Why? As though they were just not the same at all. It changed people who were normal and ordinary all week long so that on Friday, on Friday they assumed an otherness that was astounding to behold.

TGIF or whatever, even today, I still find Friday the day of the whole blessed week most filled with *joie de vivre*. It is a day on which I not only count my blessings but see them. More clearly.

12

Nosisa

Three sagging strands of barbed-wire fence around the L-shaped building; except, at a closer look one sees that where the two arms of the L should meet, there is a gap and these are, in fact, two buildings, one slightly longer than the other. But from the gate they look like one continuous building, L-shaped.

This is a school and the gap affords a pass between the front and the back. The shorter arm is nearer the gate. It is made up of two rooms, the Standard Five and Standard Six classrooms. These are the two most senior classes at this school, which is a higher primary. Standards Three and Four, of which there are two classes each, are in the longer arm of the L. These four classrooms are also more congested and noisier than the two at the base.

The gate is never closed, day or night; it stands wide open for the simple reason that when the school was built that is how it was left: just the posts.

A little path of bricks, half-submerged in the sand, leads from the gate. The courtyard is sand, never having been paved. In front of the classrooms is a verandah: a high stoep of cement over which slopes a zinc roof. For assembly, teachers stand on this raised ground as the pupils, like cattle at a dip, raise a pall of dust from the sand at their feet. That is, in summer when the days are sun-drenched, bright, and rain free. In winter, the courtyard becomes a quagmire of competing dams of varying shapes and sizes, each bent on outdoing the rest in trapping as much debris as possible, harboring as many frogs as it can attract, and making it nigh impossible to gain entry to the classrooms. Then, assembly is usually skipped: teachers conduct prayers and make announcements in their own classrooms.

Here and there a patch of flowers straggles valiantly against the inhospitable soil, brutal winds, lack of facilities and absence of a caretaker. There is even a rockery but it is not doing that well.

Behind the classrooms is an open space where, to one side, two upright H's break the monotony of the barren waste. The H's face each other, thirty-something yards apart. This is the school rugby field. A glance to the other side of the yard shows two netball goalposts. On formal sports days, when another school comes to play, these fields are marked afresh with a sharp stick or spade. Ordinarily, the children plough the markings with the heels of their upturned bare feet. All this is framed, way, way back, by a low, brooding sky, unmarred by any man-made structures. This place is tarnished by neither industrial buildings nor high-rise dwellings. African townships boast squat, single-story houses that sprawl as far as the eye can see. No thought of maximum utilization of space went into their planning. They were made for a dwindling labor pool. And the schools built for the children of those labor units reflect the planners' motive: the laborers' presence was temporary. So this is a typical school for African children in the age group, ideally, between eleven and fourteen.

Six classrooms, six teachers, eight hundred pupils. This was the situation of Makana Higher Primary School in Guguletu. There is nothing particularly noteworthy about it for this is how it was designed to be. The standard features: inadequate space (inexplicably, despite government wishes, the numbers continued to grow), cement floors, broken desks, weak lighting, poor ventilation, low teachers' salaries, no feeding scheme, no government grants to translate into books, laboratory equipment, recreational and other resources; in short, sub-economic funding. All this was in keeping with the government's three-tiered system of education whereby real and sincere attempts at education were made only for the white child, with the child classified "colored" getting consolation fare and the African child trained to be a human bonsai; dwarfed in mind and soul in complete accord with his or her shrunken body and evaporated aspirations for any future worth the name.

In the Standard Six classroom, two broad avenues of light streamed through the windows and partitioned the room into five alternating strips: shadow, light, shadow, light, shadow. Each strip annexed unto itself rows of desks on which uniformly unsmiling youngsters sat, and each row thus cast, whether in light or darkness, matched the color of its paint: the faces under light somber and those night-washed, gloomy.

The air was dense, the smell of the boys dancing on the cliff of manhood thick. And the teacher's whip of a voice cracked often to keep his wards on the narrower lane of attentiveness; a task twice tricky because of the hefty lunch his brood had gulped down during the half-hour's recess just passed. *Vetkoek* and *frikkadel*, five cents a piece, from Mama Magumede.

Like a new shilling in a purse full of old pennies, one girl stood out from the rest of the class. Clear-eyed, skin soft as velvety petals kissed by morning's dew, she sat up straight, her body, lithe as a doe's, in crisp clean and comfortable clothes, the school uniform: black gym dress, white shirt, black girdle, black shoes, black blazer, and white socks. She was the only one in the whole school who wore the complete uniform . . . every day. Her name was Nosisa.

The Standard Six teacher, Mr. Mabandla, stood at the far wall near the blackboard. As the timetable pinned at the back of the door announced, this was a geography lesson: it being the first period after lunch and the day, a Friday. Against the blackboard hung a large map of The World. Like the defenseless, kindly face of an old man, the map wore graceful signs of time: creases, wrinkles, and faded spots in no particularly discernible pattern. Out of the teacher's right hand, like a natural extension, grew a quince switch. Just short of a yard, the switch was sturdy but supple, the last the result of having been stripped of its bark and then soaked three days in salty water for extra sting.

"Lindiwe!" Crack of a voice and thunk of switch hitting the map coincided and melded as sound split airwaves.

Up jumped the girl who was thus summoned. Her eyes she fixed on the point where the switch rested, gathering strength for its searing leap. She swallowed hard several times and rather rapidly. There was nothing in her mouth except her fear and what it brought. Her whole body taut; her ears were amplifiers, ready to pick up the barest *soupçon* of sound.

Three rows to her left, Nosisa, popular with teachers and pupils alike, tongued the single word: "nigh jar"; ejected from deep down her throat. It came out in two slow, long lines of sound: "nigh jar." Nosisa's lips perfectly immobile, were barely open.

"The Niger, sir," gulped Lindiwe. She prayed she had heard correctly, that she said the right answer.

Slowly, hesitatingly and gratefully, she sank onto her seat, sensing rather than being absolutely in the know, that the response she had given was the desired one: correct.

Lindiwe's immediate neighbor, fearing she was next, began shaking violently. Dudu's baby-elephant body moved in numerous ripply mini-waves. Visible through the serge gym dress she wore, and the blouse, the sweater, and blazer; the tremors traveled in invisible waves from her mountainous folds onto the wood she sat on, and snaked across its grain to where Lindiwe sat. A rabid dog on a cold night couldn't possibly shake more, thought Lindiwe, trembling from the little shock waves of her neighbor's nervousness. Dudu had all reason to be fearful. Unless the teacher, by random selection, sprang a surprise on his next victim, she was next.

Nosisa, big eyes following the teacher's every move, fought off distraction. Teachers often pounced on her. They said she disrupted classes. Was it her fault she was bored most of the time? Today, however, the thought did not amuse her.

Dudu was the oldest in the Standard Six class. She was also the fattest pupil in the entire school; no mean feat in a school that size and a class of a hundred strong. However, her distinction did not stop at those two characteristics. She was at the bottom of her class; and this made her well acquainted with the teacher's switch. In all its biting suppleness.

As the geography lesson came to an end the boys rushed off to "Handwork" while the girls remained at their desks waiting for Mrs. Boya, the needlework teacher. The girl who knew all the answers was deep in thought. Boisterous and chatty usually, today Nosisa was quiet and filled with a silence her classmates did not understand. "Are you sick?" Sindiswa asked her friend for the second time that afternoon. Nosisa merely shook her head.

As he left the class, Mr. Mabandla had another map in his mind. From the highest peak to the lowest depth — that is how he thought of them. Today, however, his peak was overcast: what is the matter with the girl? Nosisa had not been herself today, he mused, walking away to his next class.

He would have been even more surprised than Dinga, a boy who fancied himself in love with Nosisa. Daily he tried to get her attention and daily his attempts were repulsed. Nosisa not only gave him no encouragement, she was openly hostile. "I'll tell on you." Or, "Don't be a fool." Those were her kinder rebukes. And here, today, she had actually paid him no heed . . . even when he'd touched her, putting his arm around her waist. Nosisa had merely looked at him . . . well perhaps not really looked. Dinga didn't know how to describe what had happened. Sure, her eyes had met his, were directed his way . . . but, he had seen something he had never seen before, something he didn't know. It was as if the sun gave off light . . . only, with no warmth and there was not even one beam coming from it. As if the sun were dead. That is how Dinga thought of that look. It was as if Nosisa's eyes were dead.

Mrs. Boya seldom had to correct Nosisa's work. This day was no exception. When time came for her to show her work, the only remark the teacher could make was: "Look how neat her work is. Look!" And she actually called out several culprits by name saying, ". . . whilst you put yours under the bed or in the pigsty overnight." Nosisa went back to her seat leaving Mrs. Boya wondering why the girl was so quiet. Even her famous dimply smile had taken the day off, it seemed. However, Mrs. Boya's mind was called to higher duty, pupils whose work made her want to cry. Long had she said were it not that the Western Cape was a Colored Preferential Area she would have sought a job as a seamstress. But Africans were not allowed to do those jobs in this part of the country. Clerical and skilled labor was set aside for colored people, according to those who made the laws. So there was nothing to do but to go on teaching.

After school there was sport, choir practice, and cleaning. Those who lived "far," which meant in the suburbs where white people live, were excused from these extra-curricular activities. Even school principals feared scrutiny from white people. Any white people. And the families where such children as Nosisa lived with their mothers where the mothers worked as domestic servants, were white.

"One and two, Gumede," Nosisa said quietly, handing the vendor fifteen cents. She accepted the *frikkadels* and a *vetkoek*, tore the *vetkoek* open and stuffed the *frikaddels* inside.

Magumede was rather fond of the girl. A respectful child, she was not like most of the children, ragamuffins who wanted *vetkoek* without paying cash. Also, she never argued like the others, "It's too small," "It's not fresh" or any other such nonsense. Magumede was glad the girl had started buying from her.

Two years ago Nosisa had won the freedom to buy her own lunch instead of carrying it from home. She, like all the other children, enjoyed robust ribbing from Ma'Magumede. And now she made a heartfelt effort at smiling as the old woman laughingly asked, "Running away from your location boyfriends? Watch out for those white boys, mmh?"

A bit shy, thought Magumede to herself as Nosisa waved her goodbye and left. Magumede watched the girl walk away and shook her bedoeked head. Why is a young, pretty thing like that looking so sad? Then she stopped, telling herself she had her own worries to occupy herself with.

Mama Magumede, fat and heavy as any of the *vetkoek* she sold, was more of an institution at the school than even the principal, who had been there longest of all the teachers. One could tell the school timetable by Mama Magumede. Her cart, made from old bicycle wheels and thin planks salvaged from milk crates, fruit boxes, and other untraceable debris, pulled up at the school at exactly ten minutes before each recess.

Ten minutes was all she needed. She had, over the years, perfected her routine. She wheeled her cart, dragging it or pushing it depending on whether it was her shoulders or her back she had to nurse more that day. When she reached her corner, not too far from the gate, where some shrubs promised shelter, she pushed the cart against the warped barbed-wire fence and perched herself on her stool — an old wooden crate, LION LAGER lettered in bold black on its much scrubbed flanks.

Small break saw Magumede there, the cart laden with sweets and cool drinks and whatever fruit was going out of season and therefore dirt cheap. Lunch break she was back. This time though, the cart was filled with the *vetkoek* and *frikkadels* and, of course, drinks. And for the last break she brought light fare again. And this time she didn't bother going home but instead waited right there outside the school yard until school was over. For those who had choir practice or sports after school, she was welcome salvation.

Nosisa left the school and her friends behind, and made her way to the railway station, weighed down by a heavy heart. All her many problems pressed down on her today. She reminded herself of snippets of stories of others' suffering: Christ on the Cross; His Mother, Mary; victims of floods and earthquakes; victims of religious oppression; political prisoners on Robben Island; victims of repression and torture living under dictatorships; people plagued by drought and famine; sailors whose boats sank into the bottom of the world under the unseeable sea; victims of fire.

But the half-hour walk to the train station was a journey through the thorn-strewn tangle that was her life. Recently, the sorrow had turned inward. More and more she was having difficulty separating others' suffering from the suffering only she knew. Her private agony that not even her mother (especially her) suspected. Now, she saw, she, it was, on the cross. Nosisa, she admonished herself, that is sacrilege. But the very next minute off went her mind, the starving children of Biafra, they are better off than you, it said. They do not see what they cannot eat. But I, daily, I have Karen with me. Daily.

Recalling sorrows of the world, from time immemorial, was not difficult for the girl. Her mother's prayers every evening were never narrow or selfish. They were compassionate, rising from deep within her heart, boundless in scope. By age four, Nosisa knew of the "agony of the widow looked down upon by day and visited by untold demons in the night." She felt "the misery of the child whose mouth would never say Father." When her mother prayed, she recited the whole catastrophe that was "the burden of this life and the Way of the Cross."

Therefore, when the girl found herself unhappy, she was not much surprised. Nor was she disappointed. She had not expected happiness. She had never seen it in her mother. She had never heard her talk or pray about it. Indeed, the girl would have been uneasy had she suddenly stumbled on it herself or found herself thinking she was happy. Always a little sad for these, for their suffering, now, the pain had multiplied, it had become bigger and stronger. For in the suffering of each, Nosisa saw a little of her own. And hers engulfed her with such completeness, the girl felt she could never escape it. It went everywhere with her. Asleep or awake. It was there. After school, it took the shape of her erstwhile playmate, Karen, the daughter of the family that employed her mother. And at school, her friends, the stories they told her, of the lives they lived, the games they played, the houses where they slept. Why, oh why, was she so different from everyone else? Nosisa anguished often.

She knew her friends at school thought she was luckier than most of them. Indeed, frequently, she told herself how fortunate she was; how much easier her lot; how, as her mother never let her forget, blessed she was. And, she was; she knew. But recently, her exceeding good fortune was a ton of bricks on her shoulders. Her friends did not know what she was talking about. She just did not feel lucky. Had they any idea what living with people was, white people at that, the baas and medem of one's mother?

The girl's gait slowed, her brow furrowed, as on and on she went. What would her friends say if they knew what her "luck" really meant, she wondered; and pictures flooded her mind. There she was, telling them, letting them know what it was to be her:

"Listen. Please, listen to me. Listen and stop envying the way I live. It is I who must envy you. Do you not see that daily, I watch my mother's enslavement? Unlike you, I have no shield in the shape of a home. Nothing separates me from Mother's work. Nothing separates her from the place where she works. It is her work, her home, and the only place where she can be. Mother is a slave and I know, for am I not, daily, witness to that yoke? Township children are lucky, truly they are, believe me. Do they daily see their mothers treated like dirt? No, worse than dogs? By the women they work for. And by the husbands of those women. By their children, their friends and their relatives?" With a start, Nosisa saw that she spoke her thoughts aloud.

At the station Nosisa stood outside the waiting-room. Again, her mind wandered away to that little-known world, the townships that fascinated her, where all her friends lived.

She remembered how, years ago, when she started school, the other children used to tease her. How strange it had been to see all the children in the school, all bare-footed. She was the only one in her large beginners' class who wore the full school uniform, carried a satchel, had all the books, packed lunch to school, and spoke English. How startled she had been, how disturbed, that every child had eyes the same color as hers. The teachers too. Every one had dark-brown eyes like her mother and herself. It was all very, very strange to the little girl she had been then.

Nosisa's mother, a widow, had always lived at her place of work. The girl was her only child. The widow, a devout Christian, was prized by her employers. As her medem was wont to brag, "Good help is hard to come by these days. Very hard. We are lucky with Nanny."

Because of the value the employers attached to their maid, they would suffer her child staying on the premises long beyond the age most white families tolerated black children in their midst: five years. For up to that age, the black children can be profitably "employed" playing with the family's little one. But once the white child reaches the age of five and has to start school, the black child becomes an embarrassment, a visible reminder of the inequalities endemic in the society. African children only begin school when they have reached the ripe age of reason, "eighty-four full months."

So Nosisa was allowed to stay on at her mother's place of work. And by the time she did start school she could even read and write and tell colors too. She could count up to a hundred, add a little, and subtract even less. But, compared to her classmates she was bordering on genius.

Yet this affirmation came a little late to unseat the feelings of inadequacy lodged in the little heart. The pain of knowing that she was not quite as good, not quite as clever, not quite as gracious . . . as that other child.

When the children at her school ooh'd and aah'd over her, be it her manner of dress, her flawless English, or some other, Nosisa managed, always, to cancel that out by recalling some lack or loss of her own . . . always, in contrast with Karen. To this day.

She had not been in school a month, that first year of school, before she came to the notice of even the principal of the school. Had she had knowledge of her mother tongue, she would have been moved at least two classes. And even with the lack of mother tongue, had times been different, she still might have been accelerated. But this was that era of Bantu Education when mother-tongue instruction was the order of the day. Therefore to promote a child deficient in mother tongue just would have been impractical. Too impractical. It was not done.

In one respect, however, school helped Nosisa. It eased the separateness, made it less starkly felt. When Karen sallied forth, in the beginning of her future, Nosisa, left behind, felt as needed as an old, broken toy.

The train came. The girl got on and found herself a seat towards the end of the compartment. No one was likely to bother her there. But, since her mood had come aboard the train with her, she needed none to trouble her. As the train sped on its way, its rhythm and the metallic noise it made, all fused and penetrated the girl's mind:

"Karen brilliant. Karen brilliant. Karen brilliant."

And when it screeched to a stop, it cackled:

"Do-o-o-mmm Nos-s-i-is-aa. Doo-o-o-mmm Nos-s-i-iss-aa."

Again and again, she heard the strange mocking voice of the train; heard it so clearly she came to anticipate the jeering at each phrase.

Increasingly, Fridays were days she dreaded. While all her classmates anticipated weekends with the excitement of horse race goers, she recoiled at the barrenness awaiting her. And now, thought the girl, I will be there within an hour. I will not escape until Monday morning. And her eyes filled.

Her mother was ironing when Nosisa got in. The girl stopped awhile at the door and watched her mother, who had not yet seen her. Nosisa could never bring herself to think of this place where she grew up as home. Clearly, it was not her home. She and her mother lived in the maid's room, the small squalid narrow thing at the back of the proper house. "Like a tool-shed" — that is how she thought of it when she allowed herself to remember their circumstance. Light never penetrated this room, summer or winter, rain or shine. It was a gloomy room, a stuffy room, a room that never breathed, that would never know any cheer. Where the proper house was bathed in sunlight — front, mornings and the side in the afternoons — their room stood chilled in the deep shadow of THE HOUSE.

Their lot, however much the girl attempted escaping it, refused to leave her alone today. Seeing her mother's bony frame bent over the table, iron in one hand, the other guiding a white shirt, straightening it for the iron, forced the knowledge of what it meant to be there, at that place where she grew up, where she and her mother lived in a crummy little *pondok* of a room behind the house where her mother daily cooked and scrubbed and polished and washed and ironed and dusted and swept. And smiled her shy little smile, her humble and never bold smile, doing all that and more. Her mother's smile was one of the things that haunted the girl.

"I'm back, Mama." She noticed the green-saucer-covered red plastic tumbler near the sink. Next to it were two side plates, one covering the other as a lid; each a different color. The plates were also plastic.

"Good, Sisi. Here's the key. And come back as soon as you've changed. Your dress is on the hanger behind the bathroom door." The mother found the key inside one of the pockets of her pink overall.

"Thank you," said the girl as the key dropped lightly onto her cupped hands. Quickly, she turned and walked out of the kitchen door. Down two steps and she was in the backyard where, a short distance away, stood the single room.

The picture of the houses around the school came to her mind now: township houses, a far cry from the house her mother cleaned, but theirs . . . houses rented by the people who lived in them. They had that much. They could keep them whichever way they pleased. And no one could come and go into their houses without their permission. If only her mother didn't have such an aversion to living in the townships. The girl had little inkling of the costs such a venture entailed. She only yearned to be "like the others."

The dark smell of the air inside the little room told her her mother had had a busy day. "Probably didn't take her rest," observed the girl with a pang. She left the door ajar. Now she opened the tiny window and a breeze blew in scented air from the garden. Instead of cheering her, the air freshening the room only intensified her dejection. She loathed this life, the way they lived. Why did her mother take it? Remembering how her mother never complained added to the girl's sense of desolation. She did not share even this with her mother. She was all alone in her misery. Her mother would never understand how unhappy she was.

Thoughts of Karen invaded the girl. Karen who already had a summer job lined up. Karen who was, even now, getting driving lessons. Karen who was wearing braces and complaining bitterly about that. It drove Nosisa crazy thinking about Karen's endless "You want to hear something, Nocks?" that were invariably followed by some information Nosisa could really do without: "I want to be a nurse. I'm going to be a physicist when I grow up. I think I'd like to be a film star." And her mother, Karen's mother, did not help: "Isn't she a dreamer, Nocks, our Karen?" Why did they think she cared about Karen's dreams? But the girl told herself she should not complain. She had no reason to complain.

Her mother never complained. Never. The girl's feeling changed swiftly. Now she was angry with her mother who never got angry and never complained. Nosisa was angry at her precisely because she never complained and never got angry.

"Mother will never ask for anything. Medem keeps telling her they can't afford to give her a raise. Likely story."

However, as swift as her anger had come over her, so did it leave her. By the time she had changed into her day-clothes and made her way back to the kitchen she was telling herself, "I should help Mother more."

In the plastic dishes Nosisa knew were her sandwich and milk. Quickly, she drank the milk and then reached down for the sandwich.

"The liquid is to chase the bread down, Nosisa." This order of partaking of her bread and milk was about the only thing that exasperated the mother about the daughter.

And because Nosisa was an obedient daughter she smiled apologetically and said, "I forgot." She did not ask, "Where is it running to?", which is what she would have liked to ask if she'd dared.

In the sink, the girl found a glass, a teaspoon, a saucer, two china side plates.

As she added her own dishes to those she found in the sink, two things happened. She knew Karen was back. Karen was the youngest child of the family Nosisa's mother worked for. Like kerosene consumed by fire evaporates, so did her noble intentions of but a minute before flee the girl. Fuming, she scoured the glass rather unnecessarily harshly and it broke. Loud clattering accompanied her washing of the dishes; it brought the medem to the kitchen.

"Sarah," hissingly she tried to keep her voice low, "how many times have I said Nocks must not help in the house unless I ask her? I don't mind if she washes her own plates. But that's Karen's favorite glass she's broken." Her tone had become querulous; but Nosisa was far from penitent.

Why can't Karen wash her own dishes? Why must I wash mine *and* hers? Aren't we both "children?" Didn't we both just return from school? Am I not as tired as she is? Of course, Nosisa had no answers to those questions with which she tortured herself. And that just made them more urgent to the girl. And more painful. All her earlier despair returned, its former fury increased a thousand times.

The unfairness of it all fueled the girl's despondency to deepest depths from which every avenue of ascent lay strewn with spiked tridents, gigantic thorns of razor sharpness, and pointed shards of the hardiest glass.

And her school friends thought she was lucky? Ha! They should see Karen. Then they would know what lucky means.

Karen. Nosisa had a litany of episodes she could recall at will. These all had one thing in common. They were the markings of real, no nonsense about it GOOD FORTUNE. LUCK. And Karen had all that.

The comparison of her own life with Karen's always left Nosisa disgruntled. Today, it plunged her into a gloom where she saw herself as not unlike Dudu or Mama Magumede . . . that is, when she put herself side by side with Karen. She was decidedly outdistanced. She would never catch up. No way.

"I hate my life. I wish I were anyone else but me. All the others do not suffer as I do."

Although Nosisa didn't know exactly when she had first known she would kill herself . . . or, indeed how she could do it at all . . . now, she knew she would. Some time (during recess?) she'd "woken up" with the bell-clear knowledge she could. Today. Some time.

Her mother would recount later, tears washing her cheeks: "I don't know when she left the kitchen. And I don't know what made me say to myself, 'Where has Nosisa gone?' But it must have been more than an hour since I'd last seen her. That was not like her. Even when she was studying for exams she came into the kitchen often — for a cookie or a drink . . . we don't keep any food in my room. Mrs. Smith says that will bring mice."

The mother left the kitchen where she had finished serving dinner. She was going to see what could be keeping the girl away so long. The sight that met her eyes ripped through her body like a storm through a field of young corn.

The eerie wail of her keening unglued Mr. and Mrs. Smith and their daughter Karen from their dining chairs and propelled them outside where their usually sedate nanny was as one demented.

Behind the maid's room, in a little clearing between the room and the hedge separating the Smith's property from the neighbor's, stood what looked like an effigy children paraded on November fifth, Guy Fawkes Day, before setting it alight. This one was alight all right.

Mr. Smith brought a blanket and beat the flames out. He rolled the kerosene-reeking form in the blanket and subdued the flames. All the while, the mother asked: "Why, Nosisa, why did you do this? Why? Why, Nosisa?"

The mother wailed long and loud. From the daughter, there came not a whimper. Through her lips escaped not a moan. Not then, nor later at the hospital where her life lingered in the charred frame for almost a month, a monstrous specter.

The girl did not answer. She could not. She was beyond answering that question . . . or any other. And her mother, to this day, cannot stop tears streaming down her cheeks when she remembers how her daughter stood there . . . still as an outdoor pestle, while the fire licked her up. The mother still asks herself: "Why did she not cry? Why did she not cry?"

13

Lulu

A new face always caused a stir in New Site Location, where everyone knew everybody else and a stranger was scarcer than a hen's tooth. So it was when Lulu Mxube came to join her family. But for me there was more, for I soon found I'd gained the big sister I did not have. The Mxubes were our closest neighbors.

She must have been about seventeen or so years old, a great age to my eight-year-old self then. Light of complexion and built with the solidness of a jeep, she exuded, in both manner and form, the robust personality of a well-brought-up country girl: she was cheerful, forthright, and fearless. And yet she had a gentleness about her that even adults remarked on. "She is a child still," they said — which I gathered was a compliment just as, "You're all grown up" is supposed to be a compliment when said to a child. That is the logic of adults for you.

Lulu came to us with gifts of games unknown and songs new:

"*Nali, nali, nal'ihashi,*
nali, nal'ihashi — Andisobe ndincame!
Ndincanywa nguwe!

Andisobe ndincame.

Ndincanywa nguwe!"

She had a lovely, unrestrained, full soprano voice, pure and joyous. And the song, about a lover pledging his horse as token of his steadfastness, elevated Lulu to that world any little girl yearns for, the world of adult love, romance, and the mysteries of adulthood. Think of it: when it was an act of exceeding nobility for a sibling to share a bull's eye or fish crumbs, here was a prince of a man giving his horse to the lady whose favors he sought. And, of course, with the insightfulness of a child, I knew not only that the giver was a man but that this was the only horse he owned.

To baffle the uninitiated, especially grown-ups, Lulu taught us a new language:

Lu*du*lu*du*, yi*di*za*da* a*da*pha*da*. (*Lulu, yiza apha.*)

Surely, it is beyond the capacity of any person over twenty to decipher that gibberish? The insertion of the d and the same vowel as in the preceding syllable, was, in our opinion, a mystery no adult could fathom.

Now and then, some detail seeped out about Lulu's life in faraway Ezibeleni, a village near Queenstown: "By five o'clock they had to have their morning coffee or I would be woken up with a splash of cold water." She had lived with relatives, a God-fearing family headed by no less a dignitary than a minister of religion. In Cape Town she was to discover that her own family had long abandoned the church. Her father, a staunch member of The Congress, as the African National Congress of South Africa was called then, was wont to say, "The white man has had his heaven right here on earth. Here in South Africa, he certainly has. And if I find one white man in heaven, ONE!—I shall say to God, 'Let me out! Just let me out!'"

Lulu was in Standard Four when she left Queenstown. She had come to Cape Town thinking she would continue with her schooling. But the family had four younger children in primary school and a son in high school. They could not afford to send another child to school, and for a while after her arrival she was sort of in an in-between place: not adult, as she did not work; but, as she did not go to school she was not a child either.

"Now I wish I had not come," she would say, looking through our school books. "I remember these sums. I can do them." Her excitement when she found work she recognized in one of my brother's exercise books made me think of her as a child, although her young woman's plump legs and her big breasts told me she was not a child. All the more reason I worshipped her and was grateful that she spent time with me.

But then I lost her. A job was found for her. Like almost all African women of her age, she would mind the children of a white family. Lulu was a nanny. She lived at her place of employment, for her duties began earlier than wake-up time. She had to see to it that there was freshly squeezed orange juice before breakfast, see to it that shoes were polished, and the children's lunch packs were packed. I envied those children and missed Lulu's stories, her songs, and her laughter. Lulu's infectious laughter was perhaps her greatest gift to me. In my mind's eye, I saw the white children rolling on the ground, happily caught in the web of Lulu's merrymaking.

On Sunday afternoons she was off duty but she had to go back in the evening. I saw less and less of Lulu; and from the little snatches I caught, her life as a working woman was not quite as I'd imagined. Her medem set the alarm clock for her. She rose at five because when she presented herself at six she had to be "spic'n span," as her medem put it. I learnt a new English phrase — spic and span. But Lulu's songs became less gay and less frequent. Her spic and span came in one of two ways: a cold shower or a basin of warm water from her medem's kitchen. Her own bathroom had only cold water. But then, as her medem put it, "you people don't know bathrooms." And she wasn't lying either. There were no bathrooms in the locations.

I don't know how long Lulu lasted in her first job. It was not very long before she was back in the location. She told me how she had lost her job. Intently as I listened to her explanations, I did not understand why the white woman had chased Lulu away from her home. "She was red in the face; crying angry," Lulu told me. I tried to figure out how she had sinned. I failed. Dismally. Today, I see the implications of Lulu's actions, something beyond my youthful ability when I first heard the story.

The people she worked for had rushed home from an evening outing, alarmed because they couldn't raise Lulu on the phone. She was baby-sitting their two small children. On arrival, they found Lulu fast asleep on the nursery floor.

"Medem was like a mad person," Lulu told me. The white woman had screamed and screamed at Lulu. She'd woken up her children, who were perfectly safe and fast asleep. "Woke them up, shook their bodies till their teeth rattled in their heads," said Lulu; adding, "Medem couldn't seem to understand the children were alive; that nothing was the matter with them. That I was the one dead tired as that was the fourth night that same week that I was stay-in."

My child's mind truly could not fathom the reason for sacking Lulu. What was her sin, exactly? Surely, it could not be falling asleep? Not in the middle of the night? Were grown-ups supposed to stay awake, watching us children through the night? I sought signs of such caring from my own parents. Needless to say, I failed. Indeed, Father's snores often preceded my own eyes sealing themselves for the night. I came to the sane conclusion therefore, that Lulu lost her job only because of her nasty medem's unreasonableness. And I hated that woman I was never to know; hated her with all the intensity of a self-righteous eight-year-old. However, like so many of childhood's fervors this, too, was but brief.

I was glad Lulu was back in the location even though I knew she was looking for another job and would be gone as soon as she found it.

She had been in Cape Town a little more than two years, I think, when her son was born. She had had three or four jobs in that period of time; which was not unusual for nannies. Lulu's becoming a mother put her definitely and irrevocably into the world of adults. She was lost to me forever. That Lulu was an unwed mother only made matters worse.

She had not only brought disgrace to her father's house but she had lessened her chances for a good marriage and diminished her *lobola*, the bride price her father would get in the event of her marriage. In her parent's eyes, as in the eyes of the whole community, she was damaged goods. My own mother put a stop to my association with Lulu. Oh, she did not come out and say: Lulu is bad and I do not want you anywhere near her. Oh no. Grown-ups don't operate that way. They are sneaky. They are tricky. They are deceitful. Mama said, "You know Lulu is going to have a baby. She will be too busy now to have time for you and I don't want you bothering her." I nodded; but not for a minute did I believe she was worrying herself about Lulu.

With a baby Lulu could not work. The baby was still drinking from her breast when Lulu's father found a solution to the problem of supporting his now-not-working daughter who had a child. A husband was found for Lulu. He was a widower with children older than Lulu.

He is a good man, hardworking, and able to take care of a wife, it was said. Everyone agreed that was the best thing for Lulu. Popular opinion had it that since she had got herself into trouble it could happen again. And while, with only one child, a man might still consider her suitable as a wife, what man in his right mind would take a woman who had a flock of children? Of course the widower was not expected to take Lulu's baby as well. There can only be so much kindness in one heart after all; and no one had suggested he was demented.

Mantsethe was a middle-aged woman who had no children. She and her husband were both kindly and generous. As soon as the plans to marry Lulu off started, Mantsethe became a frequent visitor to Lulu's home. At first, this did not strike me as odd at all. In fact, it did not strike me at all until the day I overheard Mother tell Father, "Remember, Mantsethe has never washed a baby in her life. She is learning now while the mother is still here. Also, she and the baby are getting used to each other." And even after that, to be honest, I did not get it all. Sure, I burned with curiosity. Did it mean Mantsethe would mind the baby while Lulu went to work? Maybe then she would not have to go to that awful old man and be his wife.

Thus I comforted myself, having solved the riddle all on my own. Mother had shooed me out as soon as she realized I was listening. but later and with hefty help from the talk of more knowledgeable playmates, the pieces fell into place: Lulu's baby was given to Mantsethe. Lulu was given to this man old enough to be her father. But each time I saw her, Lulu did not seem to be particularly stricken. I felt sad for her. Sad that she was being given away and to an old man. Sad her baby was being taken away from her even if he would have good parents. I felt sad she had the baby at all for that, to me, was the source of all her problems.

The time came and Lulu was made a new wife. I only saw her twice or so not long after her changed status. There had been no wedding. White weddings were for virgins, but Lulu was not given even the wedding of pastel-colored bridal gowns of fallen maidens: women who got married when they were pregnant or already mothers, or "soiled" in some other way — cracked glasses, as they were called in the community. However, despite the misgivings I had, she was even prettier; glowing with the beauty that seems to surround newly-weds. She looked radiant in her young wife's gear: a blue and white German print dress that came down to her ankles, a black cotton headkerchief, a fringed, check woollen scarf pinned around her waist, and heavy shawl over her shoulders. Any husband would have been proud to point to her and say, "This is my wife." But now her beauty had no joy. It was a quiet beauty; timid or wounded even. A melancholy, haunted beauty. Fragile.

Not long after, Mantsethe returned to the village of the Transkei where she belonged, and took the infant with her. That was the last anyone saw or heard of her. And, as far as I know Lulu never saw that child again. Everyone said it was best for all. Lulu, Mantsethe, and the baby. Especially the baby.

Years passed. I went away to boarding school. Afterwards, came the government's great slum clearance project of the early sixties. Like a whirlwind, it swept black people helter-skelter.

Communities that were well-knit and welded by ties of friendship, grief and joy shared, were scattered like chickens before a hawk. The sprawling sea of shacks where I grew up made way for a spic 'n span residential area where the government put colored people, themselves routed from once cherished and settled communities. We transplanted to Nyanga West, later called Guguletu. And I lost all touch with almost all the people I had known in New Site Location. Among those families from which I was severed, was the Mxube family.

Many years passed. One day I was at the local offices of the Bantu Administration Board where, *inter alia*, we Bantu, the government designation for Africans, pay rent. And suddenly, there she was.

Although I had not seen her for more than a decade, as soon as I laid eyes on her, I knew that the woman standing alone and apart from the milling crowd was Lulu. Strange how at the very moment I recognized her I also recognized more than I knew I recognized. Looking back now, I know there was something — something in the way she stood apart from not just the people but the air, the activity in the room, something that set her apart.

Face split from ear to ear, I strode over to her. Right up to her; pushed my face under hers. My eyes, wide as saucers, said: WELL?

No flicker of recognition.

I was so excited I galloped full steam ahead: "Hello, Lulu!"

She returned my greeting politely. Too politely. And still no answering light disturbed the sweet and gentle look in her eyes even after I gave her my name. "Hello." She did not say my name.

Thinking of the changes my own body had undergone since we last saw each other, I attempted to jog her memory: "I am Vuyo's sister," I said. Her eyes stayed vacant, two deep pools that mirrored an enormous nothingness.

Swift as a magician's trick, excitement gave way to agitation. "My mother is Mantumbeza. We lived near you at New Site Location. Don't you remember me? Liziwe. Liziwe!" I repeated my name as if by so doing it would write itself in whatever lay behind those frightening eyes, that looked at me and yet did not look at me; eyes that did not look at anything at all, empty eyes.

By this time my voice had shot up several decibels. I desperately needed to penetrate the dense fog I sensed and feared without knowing what it was. I recited our former address. I hollered my father's name. I scoured my brain for clues. Anything that might trigger a response or remind her who I was. Remind me who I was.

The woman who should have been looking at me smiled sweetly but still said nothing. She said nothing at all.

I was certain I wasn't making a mistake; the woman I was talking to was Lulu, although judging from her manner of dress and her general appearance life had not been that kind to her. Her clothes were not dirty or torn; they were just not the kind of clothes anyone would wear. Not that they were unfashionable or anything like that. But the mix was all wrong. The skirt said *voetsek* to the blouse which was busy saying go to hell to the sweater. Nothing belonged together.

Yes, now that I was looking at her, really looking, I saw. Nothing worked. I saw a retarded child. I saw an elderly person, frail and helpless. I saw a stroke victim. No one who could dress herself would put on clothes such as those Lulu had on. Yet, around her dimpled cheek there hovered the slightest hint of a smile; a mere memory perhaps put there by some cells or muscle over which she no longer had control. I say smile although that is too grand a name for what may or may not have been there. And, whether or not it was a smile, between it and the eyes there was absolutely no marriage, no sympathy, no synchrony. She smiled, if smile that was, looking through me into nothingness.

I shuddered, a snake slithering down my spine.

Just then I noticed a woman approach. Recognition was instantaneous. "Liziwe! Liziwe! Where have you sprung from?"

"Lulu doesn't remember me," I said in answer to her greeting. There was no way I would not have recognized Lidia, Lulu's youngest sister. She had gone a little plump, but except for that she was the Lidia of old. She was done paying rent or reporting a blocked toilet or fetching mail; now she had returned to get her Sis' Lu so they could go home. On hearing what I said, Lidia stopped short and looked at me. Her eyes clouded. Then quietly, in a tired, faraway voice, she said:

"Oh, you don't know? Ever since the 1960 riots she has not been all there." Her right index finger touched her head. I nodded, eyes filming.

By the time we parted, Lidia and I having talked about Lulu as if she were not there, talked about her while she went on wearing her ghost of a smile that was no smile, I had the answer to why Lulu did not recognize me. Why she would never recognize anyone again. But the question to which I have still found no answer is: Why?

Lulu had been one of hundreds of people the police had arrested during the riots. She just happened to be where the police were making a swoop that day. No one knows what who did to Lulu while she was in custody. But when she came back, exactly three days after she had been taken by the police, she had become the empty-eyed woman I saw that summer day in 1975.

14

It was Easter Sunday the day I went to Netreg

Brakes grinding in protest, the blood-red Volkswagen lurched to an uncertain, shuddering stop outside our gate. All cars lurch drunkenly in Guguletu, for what passes for streets are nothing but pitted, dirt-covered trails pockmarked with ditches, and potholes so big a full-grown man could drown in one. Stock still I stood, looking out of the window opening of the one-room shack I shared with Makhulu, my mother's mother.

A full five minutes I'd been waiting for the car; alerted of its arrival by the chorus, "Imoto! Imoto!" Shouts that painted a clear picture in my mind: bare-footed children panting alongside the car; galloping as I had done so many times. And not that long ago.

Until the car leapt right into my eyes, I'd been standing on the coir mattress on the floor staring out unseeingly. In the harsh glare of the unafraid, early afternoon autumn sun the opening was not unlike a gouged eye. Blindly, it stared out. And I, behind it, like some deadened nerve, mimicked. Now, the smell of the old blanket with which we stuffed the window opening at night assaulted my nose and its weight glued my feet onto the mattress.

A small, compact woman, not yet thirty, scrambled out of the car: Mother; a bright yellow-and-black plastic shopping bag suspended from each hand. Food and clothing. The invariable badge of her medem's bounty; things Mrs. Wilkins had given her out of the kindness of her big heart. Too bad she had the body of an elephant in the family way; only Makhulu wore the clothes Mrs. Wilkins gave Mama. Makhulu didn't mind folding, pleating, and wrapping the voluminous garments around her own far from substantial frame. Mother, stooped under the weight of her employer's goodness, walked slowly from the car towards our shack. I watched her, and knew that the fact that today Mrs. Wilkins's beneficence stretched to include even me, personally, weighed heavily on my mother's heart. The same knowledge paralyzed me.

'Khulu, who had as usual been hovering around it, opened the door for Mother.

It was Easter Sunday. Three days before, Mother had said, "Mrs. Wilkins will come with me on my next day off; Sunday." I was ready long before they came. They were taking me to Netreg. Netreg (which means justright) is a colored residential area not far from Guguletu where I live. Guguletu is an African township.

"Are you ready, Linda?" I knew she had not put the bags down. I would have heard the "table," a plank nearly a yard long, sighing. The "table" sighed each time it had to find a new way of balancing itself on the empty kerosene cans on which it rested. I understood its disgust. I, too, had my sighs; but I kept them to myself.

"Is that how you greet these days?" asked Makhulu, clearly piqued.

First, the rustle of plastic as bags exchanged hands, hit me. A few seconds later, the smell of fried fish enveloped me; blocking my air passage. I gagged.

"Oh, I'm in such a hurry. I'm sorry, Mama," replied Mother. She had come nearer where I stood, I could tell from her voice. The linoleum on bare sand floor did not make much noise. But I knew she had come closer. I froze.

She lifted the "curtain," a tired, discolored damask tablecloth sporting interesting tears in varying shapes and sizes. It was, no doubt, bequeathed to us by some white family for whom Mother or 'Khulu (for she used to be in the same line of work in her younger days) worked. Behind this, was my place: the mattress on the floor, a cardboard box with all my wordly possessions, mainly school books. A thin, bare wire hanger drew a dull-gray outline on the newspaper-plastered wall where it hung forlornly from a crooked, rusty nail.

"Come." And, ffwhissh! I heard the curtain fall and sensed her stalking away. I turned and looked at the spot where, I fancied, she'd stood a second ago. The dumb "curtain" stared back; and I pictured her stalking back to the car. Once more, my eyes flew to the window opening; but my feet were still cemented onto the mattress on the floor.

I did not move. But my heart jumped forsaking its seat and went and plonked itself up my throat making breathing difficult. A cold blanket wrapped itself tightly around all of me as it coated every inch of me inside. I was turning into Lot's wife, in ice.

There was Mother getting back into the car. "Come." One word. And all the fear I had ever felt since I was born collected itself into a ball of writhing worms at the pit of my stomach. COME, said the ball turning and turning in my stomach.

I was not surprised she had said no more to me. I did not expect her to be fussing over me. But Mother's one-word command stabbed my heart and jellied my already wobbly legs. I do not know how my feet managed it, but they must have done so because I was saying "Good afternoon, Me'm" to Mrs. Wilkins as I slid onto the seat behind her.

"Linda," scolded Mrs. Wilkins, "when will you stop calling me Medem?" She was smiling her brown teeth smile to show me she was not angry. She wanted me to call her by her name, Sue. But, to this day, I don't know how to call any white person by their name. It is not done. Besides, she was older than my mother. So, I mumbled, "I'm sorry," and just in the nick of time, stapled my tongue to the roof of my mouth. I'd nearly said "I'm sorry, Me'm."

Me'm Sue started the car and we were on our way. Unconcerned, the car grunted and tottered while a group of children, in varying states of nakedness, sprinted alongside it. Lithe mahogany limbs glistened announcing some mothers had had the Vaseline and time to scrub their offspring. One little fellow caught my eye. He was shaven so blindingly clean the sun bounced off his head as if it were a mirror or a miniature glass dome. He was clad in a torn, once-upon-a-time-white undershirt. Absentmindedly, I noticed that he'd grow to be a fine-membered man one day; for beneath the torn, scant garment dangled definite promise. That, or he badly needed to wet the grass.

I forgot . . . As the wonder of the ride filled me, I swelled: I was a passenger in a real car, a moving car. Then, glonk! went my heart as I remembered why I was in that car and where it was taking me.

Netreg is about ten minutes from Guguletu, by car. On those few occasions I had traveled to Langa or Cape Town I had seen the houses of Netreg, for the train passes through the township. But I had never set foot in Netreg (or, for that matter, any colored township).

It's strange how ten minutes can be such a long time. That was easily the longest ten minutes of my life. What would it be like? Netreg itself as well as the reason I was being taken there? How could I be doing what I was about to do? And Mama? What was Mama thinking of me right now? Would things ever be right between us, ever? What would Mrs. Wilkins think of me? What would she think of poor Mama? All these questions raced through my mind robbing me of the joy that should have been mine on the occasion of my first real car ride.

Briefly, once more, the thrill of the ride seduced me. Oh, I had been inside an uncountable number of cars: that is, the broken bodies of cars cast off by their owners or stolen and stripped to nothing anyone in their right mind would attempt to salvage. Wrecks were a penny a dozen throughout Guguletu. But this was different. This was a living car. And not only was I in it, it was moving; going; VRROOHM! Actually taking me somewhere. My first car ride!

I was a Standard Three pupil at St. Monica's Primary School, the only Catholic school in Guguletu. The uniform, a badly cut dress the color of bile, a sickly yellow-green, was the only decent article of clothing I owned. Hence the unclad hanger I'd left behind, a grotesque shape blotting out part of a large smiling face belonging to an African woman hanging clothes washed "WHITER than WHITE — in OMO — OF COURSE!"

Any hopes of a few additions to my wardrobe had long been quashed:

"That woman I work for does not only pay me better. She is a person. She knows I am a person." What did it matter to Mother that the women she worked for had no children? That I would never get any hand-me-downs from her? Who can blame me for being so angry at Mrs. Wilkins? All the possible cast-offs she had deprived me of: dolls, shoes, dresses, jerseys, to name a few. And then she wanted to tell me we were friends, equals, "Call me Sue!" Not me; she wouldn't get any Sue from me.

During the short journey, I sat behind Mrs. Wilkins driving her red Beetle while Mama sat kitty-corner to her and the empty seat between us yawned, a *donga* neither she nor I would ever be able to ford; for that was the last day I would be a child.

It was also the day, although I didn't know that at the time, that would affect my whole life as a woman. Looking back, I am amazed at how normal a day it looked: gay, even.

Three weeks before, St. Monica's had played a game of netball with their arch rivals, Bulelani Higher Primary School. Bulelani is in Langa. And, for us therefore, this was an away from home match on two accounts: Langa was hostile territory.

For me, however, that match was to be the beginning of the new me. Or should I say the old me? The new me, whatever else she is or isn't, is very, very old: older than any living person I know.

And the day I went to Netreg is part of the birth of the me who I became that day. Although, on second thoughts, perhaps it is not fair to blame it all on that one day.

Perhaps it all started when I was born. Or in Langa that day we played Bulelani and they clobbered us ten-zip; an unprecedented wounding. Or, perhaps it is all a bad dream.

At Netreg we had a little problem finding the address Mrs. Wilkins had been given by one of the women in her rap group, feminists. Thanks to her smattering of Afrikaans, Mrs. Wilkins was able to ask for directions and we finally made it to our destination. As we trooped out of the car, my last netball game flashed through my mind.

I played center. And, usually, I played a game both defensive and offensive: feeding my shooters and blocking the ball from getting to the wings of the opposition. I was an enthusiastic, energetic player who threw herself completely into a game. And early on in the match that was to change my life I'd done exactly that.

Now, as we walked uncertainly to the house whose number was written on a scrap of paper Me'm Sue held in her hand, the sickening feeling born in me the day of that match returned.

Fifteen minutes or so into the game, the Bulelani center shot the ball towards the wing nearest her posts. From the wing, I knew the ball could only come back to her or, with luck and skill, go straight to one of their shooters. Aiming at reinforcing our defenses, I went for the shooter positioned under the post; she had stepped out of the circle where I could not go.

Sure enough, the wing sent the ball flying to the shooter: a high, slow curve. I crouched, waiting. Then, like a spring, uncoiled as the ball began its descent; timing myself to grab it above the outstretched hands I knew would materialize. Grab it before they reached it, or bounce it right out of their fingers. That was my plan.

Three clear feet from the ground and, WHAAM! I'd made contact with a flying rhinoceros. At least, that is how I felt.

BOOM! I hit the ground. Flat on my face. I lay sprawled; certain that never again would I be able to move even a finger. Total paralysis.

Then, movement. A tumultuous, agitating protest. Inside my belly. A frightened, turbulent fluttering.

For a moment I thought the ground under me was heaving. And then, beyond doubt, suddenly and with utter searing clarity, I knew.

I was pregnant.

No one had ever told me babies move before they are born; move in their mothers' wombs. But that stirring told me all I did not want to know. After all, I was only nearly fourteen.

That was three weeks before Easter Sunday. I thought Gran would kill me. You see, she raised me from the age of five when I became too old to stay with Mother at her place of employment. Mother has always worked sleep-in. That helps a little bit with accomodation.

Till every hair on my head has turned snow white, I will never forget the look Gran gave me when I told her. Naked contempt stared at me as at a monster. If a look in the mirror had shown me I'd sprouted a second head, I would not have been surprised. And then when she started wailing: the frail but piercing wail women make when someone has died. And then the insults had rained.

That day I finally learned something of the father not frequently mentioned.

"What am I crying for? *Yhuu! MaTolo!* What am I crying for?" The anguished call to her ancestors brought a swift, brutal answer through her miserable lips: "What did I expect from a she-dog's illegitimate child?"

What had happened to the hero who was felled by the heartless boers during the 1960 riots? But the kindly old woman who had been love itself to me was not quite done. Like a venomous snake, she hissed: "Doesn't a she-dog beget another she-dog? Hee-eh?" Her face was contorted with . . . grief?

As if my own revelation had not caused enough pain, my grandmother could not seem to stop herself from dishing out further enlightenment. For my benefit: my death. Or, hers? Her face was a hideous mask of moving emotions. Hate, fear, and dire misery chased one another; flitting across the kaleidoscopic landscape. Her eyes, florets of pain that had looked into her grave and seen the bones of the fruit of her womb, generations to come. In a voice I did not recognize she went on:

"Your mother was a child herself when she went and spread herself at the zones. I never even got any payment for damages from that man. Indeed, I do not know his face because as soon as he knew that the she-dog was riding with his pup, he did what all these men from the zones do. Went back to his village and made sure he never again took a contract to Cape Town."

The zones, euphemistically called Single Men's Quarters, are barracks used to house African men forced to leave their wives and children in the village when they get "permission" to come and work in the cities. That most of these "migrant" laborers were very much married bothered government policy-makers not at all. It could not. The white, highly specialized and learned officials had yet to grasp the simple fact of these men's being human too.

The father of the child I was carrying was such a man. But that did not worry me. He had assured me that he wanted to meet my parents and not only pay damages but pay *lobola*, the bride price. When I'd told him about my father he was all concern. "Your poor mother," he said, "all alone, bringing you up by herself." He wanted to make me his wife. We had talked about this the night of the net-ball match. But, with Gran's ranting, I decided to wait until Mother's next day off.

That Sunday, my world did a crazy higgledy-piggledy and has not righted itself since. I doubt it ever will.

Mother had arrived a little after lunch. The kettle had not boiled before Gran gave her the bad news. But, although I knew I had done wrong and hurt Mother a lot, I was convinced when I told her of the willingness of my man to shoulder full responsibility she would feel a little less hurt; grateful I would not become an unmarried mother.

As is the custom when things of this nature happen, several male relatives were summoned. These would be men of the Tolo and Bhele clans; Makhulu's and Mama's clans. The clan ensures our survival. Everyone belongs to a clan and because of that, no one can ever be without kin. When we introduce ourselves, the clan name is of more importance to us than the last name for marriage within the clan is taboo. A complete stranger becomes a brother or sister when it is found that he or she is of the same clan. I was being brought up as a Bhele since my own father had died before I was born and I had had no connection with his people. Now, our relatives had come to assist kin in distress. It was decided to waste no time but go, that very same day, to discuss *lobola* with the culprit. I would accompany the party, for that too is the custom.

Mother, either not trusting these men to represent her capably or at Gran's instigation, I never found out which, decided to come too. Up to this point, everything seemed to be going according to plan.

"And these white people don't listen to us when we tell them it is not right to put all these 'single men' so close to our families." This came from the most senior of the men on realizing that the zones were where we were headed for. Fearing repercussions, I had not volunteered this information earlier on: there is a name for women who frequent the zones.

I had warned Mteteleli we were coming; so he was expecting us. He was not a boy by any reckoning. But he was also not old. We had never discussed things like age but I knew he was "proud to be with such a young, unspoilt, sweet thing." And I liked his being proud of my tender age. It meant he would never leave me, I thought. Oh, yes, young I may have been, but I'd seen and heard enough of life to know that men did tire of women. Therefore, I saw it as advantageous that I was young enough for him to like it.

The visit to Netreg is vivid in some respects, dull in others. All I remember of the face of the woman who opened the door to our knock are the crow's feet etched around her eyes. Her hair, streaked with gray, is pulled harshly back into a matronly bun at the nape of her neck. I remember being taken to an inside room, a bedroom I think, although what makes me think that, I do not know. I dimly recall seeing some furniture in the room but when I close my eyes now and try to see then, the room is blurred, empty except for the thick-set woman whose flesh sags every which way, like an aged wrestler's.

Neither do I recall whether she spoke to me in English or in Afrikaans. Indeed, did she say anything at all or did she make gestures; point and show me what to do? Did she smile? frown? or was her face barren of all expression? For whatever reason, all this has been banished from my mind.

What I do remember has never left my recall. On the other hand, what I have forgotten, I forgot with amazing swiftness: inside a week, and it was all gone. Moreover, it has remained safely tucked away. It doesn't haunt me. And for that, I am truly grateful.

What has stayed obstinately with me, like plaque to rotting teeth, are the sensations grooved into my heart, deep, deep inside my heart.

She had spread the newspapers on the floor. We were alone in the room, my mother and her medem had remained in the outer room. I remember a bowl of innocent-looking water, soapy water. She dipped her hands in it. Then she made me open my legs. Wide.

A wet hand touches me. Warm. I remember thinking: Oh, that water in the bowl must be warm, because of that. She forces a cold, smooth, slippery object into me. Although it is much smaller than a little boy's penis it snags, only for a second, however. Then coldly and stiffly it glides into me. Deep into me. I arch my back; expecting pain. My eyes are closed tight as a spoiled clam. I hear the grinding of my teeth. An elusive smell wafts softly up my nostrils.

Is this all? I begin to wonder. I begin to relax; the anticipated pain has not come. I start thinking this is one of those cases, where collectively memory multiplies the experience. I must have heard exaggerated tales, I tell myself, stories far from the truth. Correction comes swift, hard and scorching; jogging the memory of my race.

This is what it must feel to swallow gasoline and set a match into the mouth. My intestines are on fire. A raging fire that pushes and swells everything inside of me puffing it up until I feel my tummy burst. I writhe; groaning. Tears wash my face. I am hot all over. Flames liquify my insides, filling me as they spread ever upward and outward and downward.

A terror-filled scream pierces my burning ears. A mad woman's scream? Or, a dying woman's?

The woman gives me a tablet. Thereafter, she calls the two people who'd brought me. While Mother helps me out of the house and towards the car, her kind employer reaches for her purse. Whether the money she gives the woman will be deducted from my Mother's pay, I do not know. And I do not care. At that moment, I doubt I will ever care about anything at all again. I am convinced I am about to die. My legs confirm this; they have already died. I can't feel them. But the ton of lead they weigh slows me; that, I do feel. The awful heaviness makes the distance, a mere twelve yards at most, a torturous trek. I feel as if some powerful evil force has come to dwell inside my body and now, for each step I take, drags me back double the ground I've gained. A century later, we reach the car.

I am alone in the back. Ma is sitting in front with Mrs. Wilkins. I'm sprawled across the whole back seat, wide enough for three. My spine, too, has died. I can't sit up. My tummy, my thighs, and every other part of me, everything is on fire.

Soon, we are home. It is not quite dark yet. "Stand up straight and walk upright." We live in dread of our neighbors' vigorous tongues. Mother does not want to give them any encouragement. She does not want them to start any gossip. She is a member of the Catholic Mothers' Guild, a prominent member. A scandal would shatter her reputation.

Late that night, an ambulance carried me to Peninsula Hospital. Later still that same night, with doctors in attendance, I lost my son, my blood.

That thieving day! My childhood gone. Forever. Gone, too, a special part of my life as a woman. Not because, years later, I would come to know that I would never bear a child. No. Not because I would never be able to have sex and enjoy it, because as a man's penis glides into me it triggers the memory of what glided out of me those many years ago. No. Nor is it the secret I carry, dark and fearful. The secret I fear will burst into full flower one day; explaining my love of washing babies — especially little boys. That is not what haunts me.

My friends know they can rely on me to look after their babies when I am not on duty. Yes, I went back to school, later on. Thanks to Sue, the feminist. She paid for my education and today I am a qualified midwife.

But she can never really buy me what I lost that day she took me to Netreg. No one can. And nothing can bring back the innocence I'd lost by the day we went there, when Mteteleli was supposed to pay *lobola* and make me his wife.

Fifteen years before, Mteteleli, then a boy of sixteen or so years old, had come to Cape Town as a migrant laborer.

Mother too has never been the same since that Sunday we went to the zones to get *lobola* from the father of the child I was carrying, the day Mother saw Mteteleli and recognized my father.

So, three weeks later to the day, I went to Netreg. It was Easter Sunday and I was almost fourteen years old.

15

MaDlomo

She looked old, very old, the first time I saw her. Old . . . and sick perhaps? Something about the way she was sitting. Something about the chair on which she sat. Or, was it her looking like she'd grown from the sand, sitting so perfectly still you doubted she breathed?

We had just moved to NY 72 and I was standing at the door looking out. Across the street and kitty-corner to our house stood a two-family building. It was outside one of these houses that she sat slouched on a rickety-looking chair. Her rounded shoulders stooped as if under a great weight. I remember thinking, why doesn't she take off that great big coat? Thinking, why, in fact, is she wearing a coat at all? Thinking, won't that thing she is sitting on topple over?

Yes, I think that's it. That is what drew my attention to her. On a bright sunny morning, in the height of a Western Cape summer, the sky white with heat even at that early hour, she wore a coat. A heavy-looking coat at that. Grayish brown in color, the coat would have been inappropriate even for winter. Our Mediteranean winters do not call for such protective gear. They are too clement for serious winter wear.

Then, as my brain deciphered the picture, I realized she was sitting not on a chair but an old kerosene can: a battered can, rusty, and obviously empty. It had seen better days judging from the scars of battle it bore: dents, gashes, and clumsily jutting protuberances. Yielding even to her slight weight, it had pushed itself unevenly into the sand and now squatted drunkenly, giving the woman sitting on it an air of deformity; lines not unlike a hunchback's. To protect her feet, a piece of cardboard peeped from under the great coat.

There was something arresting in that solitary figure, motionless in the sea of sand. All around her the yard was liberally strewn with debris: old cans, empty bottles, rags, pieces of paper, bones and other fossils from ancient meals. The usual things one would expect to find in a Guguletu yard unprotected as yards of slums the world over are unprotected and, like them, unprotecting. Even the dun-colored sand disclaimed any suggestion it had ever been white.

The thousand and one chores that go with moving soon pulled me back into the house and for some time I forgot all about her. Between placing things where I felt they belonged in the new house, trying to make the same-looking dreary Guguletu house different, stopping my baby's loud mouth with my breast, and making sure there would be food when the other children returned from school, there was little room for dreaming.

It was well towards evening that same day when a knock sounded at the door followed by, "*Angangen'uMaDlomo?* May MaDlomo enter?" "Come in," I said going to the front room. Standing at the open door was the woman of the chair.

With a start, I saw that she was far from old. Middle-aged perhaps, but definitely not old. Thin to the point of emaciation though, I observed.

"Come in! Come in!" I said when I'd found my tongue. She stepped inside, for she was still standing at the door waiting for me to invite her in. I waved her towards a chair and, for the second time that day, found myself amazed by this woman.

There was something regal if fragile in her walk. Carrying herself erect, she walked slowly and as carefully as if she were balancing a basketful of uncooked eggs on her *doek*-covered head. She reached the chair and, as gingerly, lowered herself onto it.

In a husky voice, low and well modulated, the voice of a singer, she told me she was MaDlomo from across the street. I told her I had noticed her sitting outside in the early morning.

"You haven't been out since the morning then? I sit outside all day long, not just the morning."

Perhaps the envy I felt at such freedom painted itself on my brow; I don't know. But after a slight pause MaDlomo added, "T.B., you know."

Astonished, I saw beauty shine through that disease-riddled face. Real unadorned beauty. MaDlomo had the most serene face I had ever seen; and years later, that sad-tinged beauty haunts me still. Gaunt and whittled features could not hide the classic arrangement of her bones. High cheekbones were crowned with luminous eyes that had the frankness seen only in the new-born or the crazed.

In the days that followed I was to verify, with my own eyes, what she had told me about her day. As wealthy retirees travel to warmer climes at the first hint of winter, MaDlomo scuttled for sunnier patches in her own yard. However, her own seasons were marked on the cold round face of the alarm clock perched on the formica cupboard in her kitchen. And they were brief; chasing each other with uncomely haste. Her chair hop-scotched stalking the rays of the sun. From spot to spot it darted; pursued by the long, cold, misshapen reproduction of the house she'd fled — the relentless shadow painted by the same sun she sought. Her day, indeed, was a dizzy round-about; a slow-motion catch-as catch-can.

She rose at first alarm when her husband rose. She left when he left for work and she was on her way to the Anti-Tuberculosis Clinic. Together they left the house and walked until they reached the junction where NY 1 and NY 3a cross. There, he turned left making his way to the Railway Station while she continued straight down NY 1, past NY 50, where the Chapel Street Methodist Church stands, until she reached the corner of NY 3. A right turn brought her to the clinic.

By the time most people woke up MaDlomo was already sitting on her chair, the empty kerosene can turned upside down and cushioned with whatever rags or newspapers she could lay her hands on that day.

Over the years I got to know MaDlomo well.

Witty, wily, and winsome; she became a regular visitor to our home. And as time passed I got a picture of her, of a past few would have guessed.

Her husband, Tolo, she had met fifteen years before I became their neighbor. They had two sons and a daughter. The boys were already in school; the little girl, only five, had two years before she started school.

They had met in Cape Town where they had come to work; she, attempting to escape the poverty of the locations of Graaff-Reinet where the only opportunity for work lay in the harsh boer farms and the word employment was a euphemism for indentured labor. And Tolo? Proudly, his wife would often say, "Tolo had come to Cape Town seeking everything but his own humanity. That, he had sucked from his mother's breast. It had been nourished by his people. He had not yet learned it was in dispute. That lesson he would get in Cape Town where he would find, for the first time in his life, that there were people not quite convinced of the black person's humanity."

They had met, these two. Young people far away from home. He had never held a pencil in his hand; and she would teach him to read and to write. "I taught him how to hold a pencil and I held his hand as he learnt to write *a e i o u* for the first time in his life."

MaDlomo sang in the Church choir and Tolo converted to Christianity. Before he was baptized, at the estimated age of twenty-five, he had no experience of organized religion. His beliefs were basic. He lived in peace with his fellow men, with nature, and with Qamata, the god of his ancestors. He did to others better than he felt they ought to do by him.

A townsgirl by the time they met, MaDlomo taught Tolo some of the joys of modern living. She played tennis. She had learned ballroom dancing. And she loved beautiful clothes. He learned to dress in the manner of a man who had been to the white people's city. Although he never became very good at it, he could swing a racket and knew how to keep the score. And he became a very good ballroom dancer by anybody's reckoning.

After a suitable length of time they had married, and in due course, had the children.

With the arrival of the first child, MaDlomo had continued to work in the white homes where she cooked and cleaned, minded the children and did the laundry.

"But, after the baby was weaned, we found an old woman here in the township. She, too old to work in the white women's kitchens, would mind the baby. For an agreed price. Thursdays and Sundays, when I was half-day off, I came to see him. That was Sisa."

Tolo was not that lucky. He could only come on those rare Sunday afternoons when there was no overtime work at the docks where he worked.

This young family needed every penny. The baby's food and clothes as well as the money for the woman who minded him — all these new costs were making themselves felt.

Still, the couple felt they were not doing too badly.

With the third child, however, it simply did not make much sense for MaDlomo to work.

"The peanuts a month I was getting as a domestic servant barely paid the old woman who minded the children. It certainly did not stretch to all the food, the clothes, and the medical care they needed. After looking at our problem, looking at it from this angle and from that angle, Tolo and I decided I should stay at home with the children. Tolo would not only take all the overtime he could get but would try to do gardening whenever possible." MaDlomo's employers were sad to see her leave: "We truly are sorry, Sheila," said her medem, "you've been with us for a long time and we shall miss you."

In appreciation for her more than ten years of uncomplaining service, the Greens gave her a white cardigan; no doubt thinking of her love of tennis. They also promised to tell their friends about John's need for gardening jobs. An elaborate useless plan was devised, for the Greens knew their Sheila did not have a phone. There were no phones in Guguletu.

Her last day at work, all her belongings in plastic bags, she was huddled into the family station wagon and Mrs. Green herself drove her to Claremont station where she could catch the bus to the African township of Guguletu. She left before the Green children returned from school. It was deemed better they be spared the trauma of having to say goodbye to their nanny who was so much "a part of the family."

"At Claremont station Mrs. Green deposited me, made a U-turn, 'Bye, Sheila!' she said and sped away waving a thin arm through the window of her fast-disappearing car.

"Me? I had to fight my way into the bus and, when my stop came, jostle my way out of it. I tell you, the bus was packed, the buses are always packed. This day, though, my task was made a little more difficult than usual by the cumbersome bags I was carrying. And, wouldn't you know, some of them, of course, chose to regurgitate their contents onto the bus floor."

That same afternoon she had gone to pick up the children and later that night Tolo had returned home. It was the first time in their marriage that they had spent a night under a roof not of the back house or out-house of some white family. They had been married thirteen years and had children aged twelve, nine, and five.

"After that I became the dog you see today." With time I came to recognize her many moods. This confession meant she had no money. Never one to beg, MaDlomo would do the laundry or the ironing, scrub the house or mind the children while I dashed off on some errand. She was always scrupulous in whatever task she did, but as soon as the money hit her palm, off she was to the nearest shebeen.

"My mother died, and I could not go to the funeral. I did send some money to help with expenses though. Then my father died, and I didn't even have five lousy rands to send home." That day she would not touch a drop. But the volcano would erupt, spewing scorching tales of attempts to make ends meet, attempts that were systematically thwarted; the ends stubborn, unfriendly, and categorically refusing to meet.

Her husband, she said, was doing his best. "But these boer dogs just do not pay us enough. They suck our blood, that's all. Suck our blood." When she'd wearied herself ventilating, a faraway look would come over her face and, carefully, she would get up and gently throw the coverlet, without which I never saw her whatever the temperature, over her shoulders. Tall, straight as the reeds of the Mzimvubu, the river from which the proud kings of amaMpondo bathe, she would spit out: "*Rhaa!*" And that expletive would be followed by the pronouncement that she was of the Dlomo clan, one of the royal clans of the Xhosa people. And with that, out would the "princess" saunter, looking as if she didn't have a care in the world.

Tolo did not drink. He did not smoke. Like most new converts, he was more Anglican than the woman who had introduced him to the church. A quiet man, I never once heard his voice raised: not to his children, not to his neighbor, and not to his wife. And the last was the most surprising: that kind of husbandly tolerance is not too common in Guguletu.

"I scoured that illiterate." That comment, on rare instances, signaled that the princess had pleaded in vain with her husband and he'd refused her money to buy a drink. "What else do I get from him?" Told me MaDlomo felt she wasn't getting her due returns.

Haughtily, she claimed, "Why would I want any more children when we can't afford the three we have?" — as if she had not gone out with Tolo and other men before him, without that resulting in the birth of a child.

MaDlomo's coughing did not subside all the time I knew her. Indeed, in many respects, her physical condition worsened. I supposed whatever good her meticulous adherence to treatment might have wrought was canceled by her equally tenacious faithfulness to liquor.

Her hair fell out in big, prematurely graying clumps. Her skin, which, although beginning to wrinkle when I met her still bore more than a trace of its natural suppleness and was copper colored and blemishless, turned the color of bare earth during a drought; a parched, graying brown. It scabbed; black hairy blotches sprouting like fungus on a round wholesome loaf of homemade bread. Even her arms and legs broke out in runny sores. She had shrunk to little more than the bones that kept her up. Only her spirit remained unscathed.

"He has someone," said MaDlomo one day. And I did not have to ask for an explanation. I understood her husband had taken another woman. For a while Tolo would sneak out of an evening and return in the wee hours of the morning. "He is doing it for the children," said his wife. "He doesn't want them to know." I admired such consideration for one's offspring. Yes, I thought to myself, that Tolo is a man who knows how to conduct his business. No need to hurt the children. Let them have a childhood.

But, I don't know whether it was the expensiveness of keeping two homes or whether the other woman grew weary of being the hidden wife, but after a while this woman moved into Tolo's home which was also MaDlomo's home.

A great debate ensued in the community. The NY 72 Street Committee held a meeting. There were those who condemned Tolo for openly committing adultery. Some, however, maintained Tolo was a grown man and as such entitled to share his bed with a woman. And since his wife could no longer, because of ill health, be a wife to him in that respect, what was the poor man to do?

MaDlomo it was who put the whole debate to rest. She came in front of the Committee and pleaded her husband's case. "Do you know," she said, "a lot of men would long have thrown me out of the house?" A great many gray beards nodded vigorously, in complete accord.

"Tolo, on the other hand," continued MaDlomo, "has not only allowed me to remain in the house where I pay no rent, he gives me food and, occasionally . . .," and here a suspicious bout of coughing halted her and there was a twinkle in her eye as she went on to say Tolo sometimes dared give her some money. Many in that meeting chuckled openly, aware of the reasons why anyone would be less than enthusiastic about giving her money. It was not secret that the lady was a guzzler. And so, Tolo lived with the two women and their children, for MaNdaba had two children in rather swift succession. Both children, girls.

MaDlomo's own children were now in their teens. Handsome boys they were too; and well behaved. Their sister, although she had her father's rough and ready looks, was saved by the good humor and vivacity she'd inherited from her mother.

Long into the evening, MaDlomo would regale us with accounts of the virtues of being a senior wife. The younger wife did all wifely chores because, as the "princess" so aptly put it: "She is the one who gets the honey at night; she must sweat by day." And, on the rare occasion some nincompoop challenged or queried that self-evident truth, MaDlomo would draw herself up, disdain on each square inch of her frog-skin face and say, simply, "For years I did." And then she would toss back her head and laugh: "Haa-ha! What a fool I was." Yet, even as she said that, her eyes would be dancing away; her eyes never without mirth.

She was such a cheerful woman that I forgot she had tear glands. But, till the day I die, I will never, ever, forget the day I saw her cry.

"Mama says please come at once!" MaDlomo's daughter, Vuyo, burst into the house without knocking one afternoon. I set off with her, fearing her mother had taken a turn for the worse. Only that or worse could account for the child's behavior: she not only had not knocked but had neither greeted me nor addressed me as custom demanded. I was outside before the cold air on my hair reminded me I was *doekless* and I snatched Vuyo's jersey and hurriedly draped it on my head.

MaDlomo was lying in bed in the front room. In all the time I had known her, I had never seen MaDlomo in bed. Her face was turned towards the wall and she was all curled up; knees chasing her chin.

"Mama," Vuyo said in motherly voice, "Mama MaKheswa is here." She was patting her gently where the shoulders should have been while I stood there chilled to jelly by the utter sadness that engulfed me to see MaDlomo looking the sick woman she was.

When she still did not stir, I ventured a greeting and teased: "I can see you really feel royal today. Well, I have come; for you have called."

Still no response came. I edged nearer the bed realizing, by now, there was nothing more to do but lift the blanket and see what the matter was. "MaDlomo," I whispered, although Vuyo had left and we were alone in the room, "what is wrong?" Again silence answered me, so I went on, "Here, let me see you." I neared the bed and lifted the blanket off her head.

A bullfrog plugged one eye. And it was still growing. In a day or two she would have the king of all shiners; and I wondered whether the eye would not be permanently damaged. A crude white bandage sat feebly around her head like a sweatband. Even as I watched, red dots peeped and grew to eyelets. The eyelets joined together and became florets. Wet and growing wetter, rougeing the white around her head.

"Dear God!" I blurted. "What happened to you?"

With tears streaming out of the other eye, the one that could still shed tears, she replied:

"That witch, Tolo's wife, beat me up."

Even as I looked on, the swollen eye was getting more swollen;

angry red vying with purplish green for supremacy. Thick fluid oozed out and traced a snail's path down her planed cheek.

"Th-a-tha-at thing . . . tha-aat thing that can't even write its own name . . . that thing laid its filthy hands on me!"

The inevitable had happened. MaDlomo and MaNdaba had had a fight; over a trifle, as both would later say.

The younger wife had pushed MaDlomo and she, too weak to stop herself from a skid, sailed straight into the corner of the Welcome Dover, the coal-and-wood stove. Hence the gash on her head. The outside corner of her left eye had pinned itself on one end of the handle of the stove's door.

A neighbor who worked as a doctor's receptionist did what she could. MaDlomo flatly refused to go for medical attention. Also, from then on, MaDlomo refused food. And no amount of coaxing, no threats, not even cheap bribes worked.

I had not thought it possible MaDlomo could get any thinner than she already was. Two weeks in which she mourned her own death showed me how wrong I had been. By the day, we saw her waste away until her skin stretched taut and transparent across jutting bones that recalled illustrations in physiology textbooks.

After that first time when she told me of the fight between her and the second wife, MaDlomo would not mention the other woman: not by name nor by inference. From that day till she died, she would not blame her for her condition. "I did not marry a woman," she would retort to any mention that they make peace with each other. "I have no wife," she would add and thereafter keep her own peace, refusing by word or deed to have anything to do with MaNdaba.

In all this, Tolo was like a man caught between his wife and his mother: indecisive and dithering. The more stubborn MaDlomo was, the more lacking in firmness Tolo showed himself. He was here; he was there; he was everywhere. Except, he achieved nothing at all.

While Tolo knew not what to do or whom to blame for the abomination in his house, MaDlomo let it be known she had been let down, betrayed by loving too well.

"I have never gone back on any promise I made." No more did she need to say. What did she promise herself the day MaNdaba pushed her and she hurt herself more than we saw? Her bodily wounds, it soon became clear, were nothing to those her spirit had suffered.

Two weeks the great heart lay saying very little; preparing herself for her death.

"*Uyahamb'uMaDlomo.*" Once, she smilingly predicted her departure. The situation was too desperate for me not to take her seriously.

Then, she was gone. Officially, legally, and physiologically, that is. I sometimes think she left us the day that she was asked to bear what, for her, was the absolutely unbearable. She chose to give up.

When her death was finally announced, I think most of us who knew her were more relieved than anything else.

There he stood, a specter from the grave. There he stood, and the howling emanating from that ghostlike figure should have raised the dead. The grave was being filled, the service over, but he refused to budge. At the grave's edge Tolo tottered; hoarse sobs heaving his shoulders as he mourned a loss whose depth only then did I begin to glimpse.

After the "princess" had gone, Tolo, everyone said, was a changed man. His quietness was not that of old. A new vagueness accompanied it these days. His eyes were often red and many said he cried still for his departed wife — a terrible burden on wife number two.

At the corner of NY 1 to NY 3a, where many a morning Tolo had turned left going to the Railway Station while his wife continued down NY 1 on her way to the anti-T.B. clinic, there, one morning on his way to work, he was struck by a bus and died on the spot.

Tolo died on the first anniversary of MaDlomo's passing away.

16

Two little girls and a city

This is not a fairy tale although, I must confess, it is full of hard-to-accept facts, episodes, and occurrences. Therefore, if you are looking for amusement, stop right here, go and pull out one of those "Once Upon A Time" stories that end "and they lived happily for ever after."

It all happened a long time ago, but not that long that it should have escaped living memory. And it was so painful I decided, without knowing that I did, to tuck it all away and go on with my life. After all, it had nothing to do with me, not really, sad as it was what happened that day, at different places in Cape Town, a city famed for its beauty.

They were very young girls, both still in the first promising decade of life. Little, little girls really.

That brilliant summer's day, in Cape Town, the sun enlivened people young and old. Its long, sure rays fell on hill, mountain, and flat with equal abandon. It poured down heat and pressed clothes close to skin. In suburban flats, squatter camps, and borderline houses in townships the uppermost thought was fleeing the furnace.

"Mommy! Mommy! Let's go NOW to the beach." The cry came from Nina. The nearly-seven-year-old was making the request for the umpteenth time that day. "Please . . .?" Her big blue eyes were bright. Dark and thick lashes fringed them reminding one of the sunflower, because of the generous proportions, intensity of color and shape: almost perfect circles.

Mrs. van Niekerk smiled indulgently. "Sweetheart," she said, "your little brother needs his nap, remember? We want him to grow, don't we?" She gave her daughter a conspiratorial wink while she tousled her son's hair as he stood swaying in his walker nearby.

Nina nodded, her eyes twinkling knowingly. Very grown up she felt, helping her mother keep Timothy in line. She was a big girl, so she wouldn't fret. They would go later on to the beach. And as her mother would say, little Timmy needed his sleep so he would grow big and strong enough to play rugby. Maybe become a Springbok like Mommy's dad had been.

To encourage Timmy who, like all babies especially boys, could be awkward, Nina announced loudly, "I am going to my room to take a snooze or maybe finish the book I'm reading; I have a few pages left. Then we can go to the library tomorrow. It's the last one I must still read." However, minutes later when her mother came to see how she was doing, Nina was fast asleep.

Eight miles away another mother, baby strapped to back, was talking to her little girl. A battle was raging between mother and daughter. Phumla wanted all her clothes off. New in Cape Town, she did not quite understand that this different world forbade even children to run around in their birthday suits.

"*Hayi*, Phumla! Leave your petticoat on. And your bloomers too!" Her mother's voice was raised, stressing the importance of the instruction.

"But, Mama, I am burning from this sun." The little girl sounded listless. She was subdued by the harshness in her mother's voice. Nonetheless, her response conveyed a sufficient measure of assertiveness to make the mother smile.

Nolungile (Mother of Kindness/Goodness) Dyantyi felt for her daughter. The child must be dying from the heat, she thought to herself. But what am I to do? I can't undress her here in a men's compound. It's not decent, these men are not relatives or people we grew up with. This is not our village where everyone knows everyone else, knows his cattle, his parents, whom he married, and knows his children. We are amidst strangers here, people who do not know Phumla or her father or her mother. Yes, she is only a baby . . . but, we are among strange people.

Phumla, her little sister, Nodoli (Doll, because she was born such a tiny thing) and their mother had arrived in Cape Town a few weeks before. They were all visiting Phumla's father, a migrant worker at the Docks in Cape Town. Nolungile was nursing the hope she would return to her village expecting child number three. Nodoli was already four years old. It was time. So she had come to fetch a child from her husband. The last two times he'd been back in Gungululu nothing had happened. Her in-law, not one known for subtlety, had started reminding her that she "came to this family to increase it."

God, she was cooking. The red brick walls of the room her husband shared with eight other men reminded her of a fire. She knew she was being absurd but they were breathing dry heat that scorched her no less than if she were sitting near a great big open fire. More heat beat down on them from the flat light gray asbestos above them. Neither ceiling nor plastering intervened to protect them from the heat. The Single Men's Quarters sport bare basics: homely, they are not.

"Here's forty cents. Run to the shops and get us *sidudla* ginger beer. That will help us cool down a little."

Against the far wall stood a rickety make-shift table. Under it and fully visible, said table not saddled with anything pretending to be a tablecloth, was an array of bottles of various shapes, colors, and sizes. Phumla took an empty liter bottle from this stock and money her mother gave her. When the liter bottle came with the metric system, in the African townships of South Africa it was called *sidudla*, the nickname for a fat woman. With thin brown arms and legs sticking out like twigs from the bright pink and blue flannel petticoat Nolungile had made her for the trip to Cape Town, the little girl walked purposefully out of the room. She knew exactly which shop she was going to. Shop Number Fifteen. They always gave one "*basella*" there.

The girl stepped briskly out of her zone, across the unpaved courtyard, raw sand walked almost black, tufts of grass straggling here and there. In two minutes she was at NY 1. Briefly, she stopped to see if there were any oncoming cars, trucks, or buses. Safe. She crossed. Past the open space of the backs of the shops she trod; around the corner, and there she was. Shop Number Fifteen, the third shop after she rounds the corner.

Because of the time of day, early afternoon, there were only two customers at the shop. Within ten minutes, Nolungile and her elder daughter were sipping refrigerator cold ginger beer out of tin mugs: the little one, Nodoli, fast asleep. And Phumla had two sticky bull's eyes, the *basella*, tightly clasped in her left hand.

At about the same time, out of very different drinking utensils in a different abode, Mrs. van Niekerk and her two children were also quenching their thirst. Timothy was having his orange juice, freshly squeezed. His chubby fingers not yet adept at holding the bottle, he had to be helped frequently either to pick it up or to get the teat to find his mouth. But he absolutely refused to have his mother holding the bottle for him; vigorously shaking his head from side to side, he squealed and grunted like a piglet. His sister was sipping gingerly away at a milk shake while the mother enjoyed a tall glass of iced tea. All this, straight from their own refrigerator.

The threesome sat on the verandah. The house stood high up the slopes of Table Mountain and Colleen van Niekerk, sitting on a white cane chair, looked down on the blindingly blue expanse of sea. Idly but full of satisfaction, she noted their part of the beach, where she liked to take the children because of an outcrop of rocks that offered shelter from the often ferocious southeaster and an immensely rich discovery field for Nina. The child liked to potter around the shallows collecting shells or simply gazing spellbound at the little things that crept or slid along the sand or burrowed into it, floated in the warm tidal pools plentiful between rocks, or nested beneath boulders. Her consuming interest and boundless patience made her parents joke they had a marine biologist in the making. "See if she doesn't get a Nobel Prize too," Piet van Niekerk would say, quite serious. The child was absolutely fascinated with marine life. She could sit still for hours watching something go about its business.

Into this reverie burst the marine biologist of tomorrow: "All right. All right. Call Hilda to come and help me with Timmy," responded the mother, reaching for the iced tea she had neglected on the glass-topped table. She was peering indecisively at the last mouthful of tea when Nina appeared, maid in tow. Mrs. van Niekerk pushed the glass away from her and said:

"Hilda, I'm taking the children down for a swim. If Master calls before we come back to tell him we will be back before six. Now can you get them ready for me? I'll go and change."

Having issued her instructions, Mrs. van Niekerk left knowing Hilda would manage. She had been with them even before Nina was born.

As the madam made her way indoors, the maid made hers around the house to the clothesline where swimsuits from previous swims fluttered in the gentle breeze.

"NO! I don't want that. I want my bikini. I don't like that thing," Nina said. Hilda put "that thing," a favorite not so long ago, on the table and reached for the baby, thinking: "Eh, this one does not have a mouth full of nonsense yet, let me start with him."

Timothy was easy on another score also. After giving him a "top and tail," changing his undershirt and diaper, Hilda put him into his waterproofed bright red little shorts. A matching cap went to cover his mop of dark hair.

The maid turned to the little miss and asked, "Are you sure now you want the bikini?" She knew from experience that Nina was not above changing her mind following similar vehemence. Only last week she had screamed her head off because her mother insisted she put on her terry robe over her swimsuit. When Madam had given up, who should change her mind but Nina. As soon as she saw her father come out of the house wearing his robe.

"Of course I'm sure. You can take that bathing costume for your granddaughter, you know I won't wear it again."

Before Hilda could say a word, in thanks or decline, Nina rushed inside the house yelling, "Mom, I want Hilda's granddaughter to have my orange costume. Mom, d'you hear me?" Back into the verandah bounded the child. Full of beans, this one always is, thought Hilda to herself. Out aloud she said, "Here you are, do you want me to help you?"

"Of course not." And although she didn't exactly stamp her foot,

Hilda was left with the impression of Nina's having stamped her foot in declining the offer.

Soon, all three were ready, Timmy in his pushcart, Nina wearing blue flip-flops, white sunglasses, a white cap with a red visor, and the blue, red, and white bikini that had caused a furor a while before. Every inch of her petite body showing the benefit of years of aerobics, the mother strolled downhill with her brood. She in crisp, white cotton which heightened her tan.

Hilda stood at the edge of the stoep and waved the trio goodbye; happy painted all over her face.

Although a not too broad street separated the Section 2 Guguletu zone from family homes, there might as well have been a concrete wall for all the interaction between children who lived in the two areas.

Another migrant child, Eleni, called out shyly to Phumla to come out to play. She had collected three empty cans — jam, Nespray, and condensed milk; the latter a little crushed from Lord only knows what of the many hazards these discarded containers face in the wastelands of the townships where rubbish collection, as all else, is a matter of others' whim. Eleni was throwing a ball, an old tennis ball someone had thrown out somewhere a long way away from the zones. She threw the ball as high up into the air as she could; clap clap clap went her hands as she ran towards the spot where she thought it would land. And all the while she kept her eye on the ball as it made its descent. She'd catch it, throw it up again, calling out, "*Phumla, yiza sizokudlala.*" (Phumla, come out so we can play.)

In a short time after these summonses started, Phumla came out of her zone and ran to her friend. "What are we playing? What are we playing?" excitedly, she cried out.

"*Drie blikkies,*" answered Eleni, assembling the cans.

Drie blikkies (three cans), as the name implies, is a game where three cans are used — three small cans, ideally not of the same size. The game demands marksmanship, manual dexterity, and speed, good eye-coordination, swiftness of foot, and the ability to dodge.

The two agreed Phumla would go first. She took the ball and went to stand a good distance away where a circle drawn by stick on the sand showed the marksman's place.

Taking careful aim, Phumla threw the ball straight at the triangular pile made by the three cans: the fat, taller Nespray tin formed the base, on top of it was the jam can with the smallest of the three, the condensed milk cans, forming the apex.

Twice she threw the ball at the cans; and twice she missed. Phumla knew this was her last chance. Each player is allowed three throws in *drie blikkies*. Slowly, carefully, taking her time, Phumla aimed. When she threw the ball, it was with less vigor but more exactness than before.

The sound of ball hitting cans came close upon that of cans bouncing off each other and onto the ground where they clattered, hitting other debris.

Phumla, seeing the ball roll away into the distance made a beeline for the far-flung cans. She swept the cans towards the little clearing they'd so recently vacated, scrambled there herself, put them together just as Eleni rushed back with the ball. "One game!" yelled Phumla victorious.

She did not make it past three games. This time Eleni returned with the ball before Phumla could build the three cans into a column. Eleni hit her with the ball shouting, "DEAD!"

It was Eleni's turn and she would not relinquish control of the game until she had a score of twelve games. That adept at dodging that even when Phumla fell upon her, ball in hand, before she had managed to assemble the cans Eleni would escape being tagged by feinting a right move and then, after Phumla had thrown the ball at her, veering to the left or throwing herself flat on the ground. Or, she would jump so high the ball went clear under her as if she were a witch riding a broom and the ball just some flotsam that happened to be in the air.

At Rocklands beach, Sea Point, Nina was also busy at play. As soon as they hit their spot Colleen van Niekerk pitched her umbrella, spread the beach towel, and put their things — sandals, sunglasses, robes and bags — on the towel to anchor it against the wind; a breeze right now but she knew how quickly that could change to a roaring towels-hurling mini-gale.

By the time the mother had everything under control the little girl was already frolicking in the breakers.

Colleen joined her daughter. "How's the water?" she asked, testing it with the toes of her left foot. In her arms she carried little Timothy, who was wiggling and wriggling, impatient for a chance to romp among the waves all on his own.

"The water's simply super. Can I go in now?" It was a rule that Nina did not go into the water unless one of the adults was watching. "Mmhh, go right in, sweetheart, I'll be here with your brother."

Nina, a strong swimmer, struck out a good few yards, turned around, waved to her mother, and swam furiously back. She played a little with Timmy, and then threw herself, face down, onto the sand.

After several swims and turns at watching her brother under the umbrella while their mother took a dip, Nina wanted to go and find "rare" shells. Any shell she had no recollection of seeing before was, for the little girl, a rare shell.

The mother watched her daughter stroll casually away. She mused: How soon she is bored with what she pesters me so much to get. Definitely, it is not for the swimming she comes here. Mrs. van Niekerk smiled looking at the graceful figure disappearing into the nooks and crannies that held so much enthralment for her child. The mother thought: Yes, she is Piet's daughter all right. Piet van Niekerk spent every minute he could spare from his busy teaching schedule at Groote Schuur Hospital at the beach. Summer, winter, and any time besides.

The crowd sparse, she could easily see Nina pick her way among the other umbrella groupings.

Nina stopped at their umbrella. Probably picking up her pail or leaving her flip-flops, thought the mother watching her daughter take off once more. But this time, Nina walked in the opposite direction from where Colleen sat, watching little Timothy chasing the waves dying on the cold, damp sand.

Also bored were the two friends playing *drie blikkies*. The match uneven, Phumla wearied of trying to catch up with her rival. She was sweating from chasing the ball, chasing Eleni who ran like a race horse, and trying to dodge the other's fatal tagging.

Luckily for this twosome, Nomalizo, another of the children of the zones, came out to play. In her hand she had a rope. So the three girls decided to play jump rope; the owner of the rope jumping first while the other two held the ends.

she benda,
she benda,
she klep,
she klep,
she omdray,
she omdray,
she set,
she set,
she lehy,
she lehy!

These "instructions," called out by the two holding the rope, are acted by the player in the middle, the jumper. The rope goes ONE, PAUSE; ONE, PAUSE; and at the pause the jumper carries out the appropriate command: bending after the "she bends," clapping her hands with the "she claps," turning around after the only of the five commands in Afrikaans, the verb, that is, "she *omdray*"; with step two incorporating step one and step three both one and two. So the sequel is JUMP-ACTION JUMP-ACTION; rope looped at pause.

If the player survives past the *omdray*, she gets to strut her stuff at the last two commands: "she sat" demands acrobatic celerity and "she lay" is always followed by the Xhosa translation, perhaps for emphasis: She lay! *Lala!* She lay! *Lala!* All rhythmical, voice and action in perfect synchrony. At this point, *she* has to jump, lie down, get up and jump again — keeping the rhythm which, for some reason, always heats up at the She Lehy!

The intricacies of this game as well as its physical demands on the player or jumper, ensure that no one girl can stay in the middle for long. For that reason, the players often lose track of time for they do not stay long enough to exhaust themselves.

Phumla was in the middle once again. Even she had lost count of how many times she had been. She was having so much fun the sun stealing westward had no meaning for her.

Meanwhile, Nina meandered among the rocks, which were not high but enough so to obscure her from view. She ranged the pools, poked about, her eyes razor-sharp keen, alert as Sherlock Holmes. In no time, she was lost to all but the beauty she saw there: dazzling colors, breathtaking shapes, and amazing activity. The little girl was at home in this world of little things; so alive, so diverse, plentiful, and seemingly never pausing for rest.

"Phumla! *Weh*, Phumla!" Nolungile screamed; her village voice accustomed to leaping from homestead to homestead, from river to field, a bit shrill in the confines of blocks of houses heaped together like anthills. She was standing at the doorway of the zone, a little concerned that she could not see her daughter, whom she had told to play just outside the door, now that the sun was setting. It was time for the child's father to return.

"Ma-a-h!" The mother couldn't tell where her daughter answered from. But from the undisguised irritation in her voice, she was sure Phumla was having a good time. A shame, but she had her own instructions, thought the mother.

"*Heyi, buya! Yiz'apha*! Hey, return. Come back here."

"Come here!" The strange man spoke in a low, quiet voice. His eyes bore into the child's. Nina had not heard him approach. Now she wondered where he had come from. She remembered the shell in her left hand: the rarest shell she'd ever seen. Even her father had never seen one like it she was sure. So delicate, like lace. And the colors, so many, so bright . . .

Almost like a reflex action, she opened her left hand, glanced at the shell before her eyes were pulled back to those of the man towering above her.

It all happened so fast: the man; letting the shell glide back into the water as she scrambled from her knees; and discovering her way blocked . . . by the strange man.

Nina, finding herself thus unable to pass, stood where she was. She thought: Where is Mommy? Will she come and get me? I don't like this man. She heard her heart thudding like the horses' hooves on her *Oupa* Vorster's farm.

"Phumla! Phumla, *ndakukubeth' ungeva nje*!" (Phumla, I'll thrash you for not listening.) "*Buya-aa!*"

One long stride, the reach of an arm, and the man grabbed the little girl, who cringed whimpering; big-eyed with fear, her mouth dry.

"*Ndiyeza-a-a!*" Irritation had graduated to rudeness. A child always addresses an adult by an appropriate name. Where was Phumla's "Mama" after the "I am coming"?

"M-mmo-ooh . . ." His hand clamped over her wide, screaming mouth so that she didn't complete the word she was screaming out.

Nina struggled. Furiously and with all her might: a day-old chick in the claws of a hawk.

Phumla's father wanted the child indoors when he returned from work. His wife, seeing the reluctance with which their daughter entered the room, crestfallen as only one plucked from a hot game can be, thought: "He doesn't know anything about children. He doesn't understand them. But then, since he is never there how would he know of such things?" Nolungile felt sad for her husband who would never see his children grow. She was sad, too, for the children, her children, for they would never really have a father. It had become clear to her that this was the meaning of the "*join*" (as the migrant labor system is called by *amaXhosa*); instead of joining families it split them into bits and pieces like the grains of the sand.

Hands of steel locked around her neck. A crunch. A moment of searing, excruciating pain. Mercifully swift, so brief the little girl imagined she dreamt it all. That's how fast it must have gone.

But the newly hatched beast had but begun his plunder. He half dragged, half carried the inert form to a thicket some yards from the pools. There, repeatedly did he maul the limp figure; fighting it although it lay still, offering no resistance at all.

"Mama, I want to play still. Other children are still out playing. I will . . ." Abruptly, Phumla's pleading stopped.

"*Mkqo nkqo! Molweni!*" The father's "Knock knock! Good evening" put an end to whatever his daughter had been about to say. Phumla was very quiet in the presence of her father, whom she held in awe.

To her, he was someone to be feared: a stranger even her mother seemed to be scared of.

Colleen van Niekerk stepped out of the water and picked her way among the sun-worshippers sprawled on the sand under the naked sun or beneath umbrellas. As she made her way to her own umbrella, unconsciously she scanned the thin crowd for signs of Nina.

Nina was not in the vicinity of the red, white and blue umbrella: a memento from a trip to Paris, it sported black bold but spindly pictures of the Eiffel Tower. So she knew she was not mistaken, that was their umbrella. And Nina was nowhere near it. Now and again she would spot a figure that looked as if it might be her but on closer look, the mother would tell herself: NO. Not her.

She walked past their spot, past the umbrella, for the child must still be seeking shells or watching a nest she'd stumbled on. She reached the forest of rocks . . . no Nina. Her skin prickled; a small army of ants harum scarum all over her body, let loose by devils she carried within her. Devils she hadn't known were there until they launched this attack. Long, thin, icy fingers encircled Colleen's heart . . . and squeezed.

The rich discovery field yielding no Nina, the mother hurried back to the umbrella. She thought: "You're driving yourself crazy over nothing, Colleen," slowed her pace, took long pulls of the salty air that had suddenly become thick and heavy. The umbrella came into view, forlorn: a deserted house.

She reached the umbrella, put Timmy down, and scanned the beach in earnest.

Timmy crawled out from under the shade and distracted the mother. Only for a moment though. She picked him up and strapped him into his stroller.

Her eyes narrowed, hand capped on brow, Colleen carefully scanned the beach. Clusters of children drew her attention. Isolated grownups who might strike up a chat with Nina. Lone figures, wandering or idling. Slowly, carefully she turned around; taking a small slice of the beach each time, pausing there and going from figure to figure in an attempt to spy her daughter, to single her out, unscramble her from the medley of humanity on the beach. She had made a full circle, and still she failed to spot Nina.

Nolungile put the kettle on the primus stove and before the water came to the boil asked Phumla to bring in the enamel wash basin from outside. She poured most of the water she had heated into the basin and added a handful of salt. Her husband soaked the weariness out of his feet.

By the time the water had cooled enough to be thrown out, he had had his first cup of tea and was ready for his bowl of *stamp 'n stoot*, stamped mealies and beans. The evening meal had started.

"Don't panic," Nina's mother said to herself, out loud. She was trying to ward off the dead-drunk butterflies threatening to awake in the pit of her stomach. She is here somewhere, she told herself; just look. Just look. She is somewhere on this beach. Get a grip on yourself.

"Have you seen a little girl in a bikini? Red, blue and white?" Her steps were long, her gait ungainly, as from group to group she hopped, starting with the neighbors and slowly expanding the terrain she covered.

"Have you seen a little girl wearing a white cap with a red visor? She's seven but tall for her age . . . have you seen her?"

She started screaming: "Nina-a-ah! Nina-aa-a! Where are you? Nina-aaa!" But no ballerina in bikini came bouncing towards her; no marine biologist sauntering hesitatingly back, annoyed at the interruption of important research. The ground had swallowed Nina.

A few people, noticing her growing distress, offered help. Little informal search groups formed and broke in different directions combing the beach for the missing girl. Soon, the stirring mounted to a whirling agitation. The lifeguard was called. Someone else called the police. And Colleen gave them her husband's work telephone number. And only then did she begin to waver in the belief she had clung onto: that Nina had lost track of time, engrossed in some observation of plant, animal, or shell . . . some enthralling "discovery" she'd come back bubbling over. But now, with police asking her questions, with police calling her husband at work, with the lifeguard scanning the darkening sea for . . . she stopped herself from completing the thought, too gruesome to contemplate. It could not be. Not Nina. Not her baby. God, not her little girl . . . she prayed without thinking that that was what she did. She prayed not knowing she prayed.

The setting sun, tantalizingly daring any who could to hold it still, hung low over Table Mountain, casting the area nestling cozily against its bosom in shadow. Like the picture of the nursery rhyme where the cow jumps over the moon, the sun readied itself to jump over the mountain . . . it looked especially radiant making its escape.

Professor Piet van Niekerk, world-renowned heart specialist, arrived within fifteen minutes of receiving the call. He was still wearing his white duster coat for he'd been in the middle of a lab lecture, his last and then he'd call it a day. In another hour and a half he would have been home; playing with the children just before dinner.

Taking his shaking wife into his arms, he listened to the story stone-eyed. Settling her back into the *kombi* where Timmy lay oblivious to the turmoil, Piet went to hear what the authorities had to say. He had great faith in the South African police.

A helicopter hovered above the beach, its searchlight peering into the underskirts of rocks, bleaching the sea colorless, and reading the vicinity with the precision of X-ray.

Mrs. van Niekerk was in shock. In someone else's *kombi*, a thick woollen blanket draped around her, suddenly her statuesque frame looked frail. She was past sobbing. One of the medicos had given her something to drink . . . that was before Piet came. She had gulped the liquid down but could not have said how it tasted. Her taste buds were numb.

Some distance from where the search concentrated, among boulders supporting scrub, a lone walker, not one of the volunteers, came upon the broken body. She raised the alarm.

From the unnatural position in which the body lay, it was at first assumed that the child had slipped and, in falling, either broken her neck or bashed in her skull. But, one piece of the bikini was gone.

Dusk had fallen in Guguletu. But there was light enough for Phumla's father to send the eager one to the shop. A little of the ginger beer remained, but it had grown tepid from the heat. And he knew the night would be long.

Empty bottle clasped under arm, money tightly fisted in, the little girl set off for the shops. Before she got to NY I, Nomalizo, she of the skipping-rope, returning from the shops tagged Phumla, who had not seen her approach, lightly on the shoulder and scurried away shouting, "*Lepi!*"

Not to be outdone, Phumla flew after her, caught up with her, touched her once on her back, turned around and fled screaming, "*Lepi! Lepi! Lepi!*"

Nomalizo hesitated. She was carrying a bottle of kerosene. The primus stove had gone out, dry. Her mother was in the middle of cooking supper. She hesitated . . . she was thinking that perhaps she should make her way home before her mother came looking for her.

But Phumla's taunts: "*Uza kulala nekat' emnyama! Uza kulala nekat' emnyama!* You'll sleep with a black cat!" got the better of Nomalizo. Who wants to be followed home by a strange cat that would then insist on sleeping with one? A black cat at that?

The toing and froing went on until Nomalizo's mother's voice rent the air: "Nomali-i-izooo! Nomali-i-izoo-ooo!", sending the culprit scurrying homeward.

Phumla, too, remembered her own mission and made her way to the shop. The pale light thrown up from behind the mountain, the last gift from the day's sun, was now gone.

At the beach, an ambulance had taken the body away. But the horror clung to those left behind. It was in their words. It was in their eyes. It was in their minds, their hearts, and in the very air they breathed. Mothers gathered their children in a frenzy, like hens spying a hawk. Coldly accusing eyes went the way of the stranger viewed with indifference or neighborly benevolence a mere while ago. All thought of fun fled with the gruesome knowledge.

The Homicide Division men had come and sniffed around, asking questions, taking pictures, and taking samples. It was very reassuring to watch them work. And disturbing to remember why they were there.

Slowly, people returned to their abandoned umbrellas that were now no longer necessary, the sun gone down — at the insistence of the police that they leave and let them go on with their work; others because they were now anxious to leave, to put distance between themselves and this place where such a thing had occurred. For a few, this strip of coastline would lose its allure for ever.

In Guguletu, human traffic around the shops was dense. School children had returned from school, workers from their toil. It was cooking dinner time. *Skollies*, knowing this, were on the prowl, huddled at shop doorways; ready to pluck any dumb-looking "chicken," as they called those uninitiated in the crooked ways of city low life.

From shop door to shop door the little figure darted. Aware she had lost time in the game of *lepi* with Nomalizo, Phumla now searched for a shop not too full of customers.

Night had closed in on the van Niekerks. They were back home; searching for new ways of being, of knowing what to do with themselves and with each other . . . living with this unfamiliar sorrow that had come into their lives. It was after eight. No one had had dinner. No one had any thought of food now. The family doctor had sedated Mrs. van Niekerk and Timothy was seen to by Hilda until the grandmothers arrived. Both sets of grandparents were now here. The four sat in the living-room, it was as if the room were empty. Complete silence. Piet, on the other hand, could not be still. He was giving orders to Hilda, answering the telephone . . . friends calling to verify what they heard on the news . . . the media . . . the cops. He looked like one who was coping better than anyone else. Now and then, a sob escaped from one of the Vorsters. And to see the heavy frame of Koos Vorster shaken by sobs was a heart-rending sight indeed.

Ginger beer bottle clutched to her chest, Phumla ran out of Shop Number Eleven and started her way home. She had just cleared the shop building when she felt the big hand mask her face. A big arm encircled her, pushing her back against a hard knee while the hand muffled her cry, robbed her of breath, and blacked out the shops and the street lights and the cars running up and down NY 1. Father? raced her mind; but instinct warned her it was not him.

Amidst screams of mothers calling children home, lovers' whistles luring partners to clandestine rendezvous, traffic noise, and blaring radios, her pitiful cry was as the bleat of a lamb during a storm. The din swallowed it up as the night hid the deed.

Grabbed from behind just as she entered the narrow passageway separating the shops from the Section 2 Offices of Bantu Administration, the little girl wriggled in vain, fighting for escape. She was scooped, thus gagged, and carried deeper and deeper into the dark shadows of the shops. And there, behind the bustling shops in NY 50, Guguletu, the man squeezed her windpipe till it crushed; silencing her voice forever. For a while, she went on thrashing her arms, hands clawing, feet kicking madly. And then, all at once, she was still; watching plump cobs of corn browning around an open fire away in her village home. The ancestors had snatched her to a safer place.

"We should try to get some sleep," said Piet quietly. "We will have a lot to do tomorrow. Let's get some rest."

Soon, in pairs or alone, Nina's family went to where they would spend the night. The Vorsters went to the guest room. Piet's parents were given his study which had a divan and a sofa. No one wanted to use Nina's room. No one. And no one was invited to.

The man in whose grasp the little girl lay did not see her go limp. He did not see her life ebb away. He had a purpose to fulfil. And set about groaning and grunting, his mouth frothing, eyes glazed, sweat pouring down his face. His shirt was plastered to his bent and steaming back.

When he was done, the shape in his hands looked like a plucked goose. Its feathers lay strewn in all directions. He saw that it had no more life left. And, utterly disgusted, the knees to chest position particularly upsetting him, he thrust it away from his blood-drenched body. There it lay, and he saw that what he had done was not good. Leaving the body unconcealed would lead to early detection. So he picked it up and rammed it into one of the garbage drums that stood nearby.

The night sky beamed and winked and twinkled with diamonds of all sizes. Some were so big it made you think you could reach up and pluck one at will. Then there were those so far, they were but mere specks glinting and glittering and smiling away, far, far away. Old, old stars that have been there from the beginning of time. And, new little ones, why? perhaps born that very same day. There they were. There they were; glorying the heavens!

Back in the zone Nolungile went often to the door and there peered out hoping to see the familiar figure of her daughter. She knew that at that time the shops were filled with people buying things they needed for the night, buying these before the shops closed. So yes, she worried a little but she was not exactly alarmed.

As time passed, however, her anxiety mounted. She was concerned that Phumla would get into trouble with her father if he went to look for her himself and found her playing. She kept hearing her daughter's footsteps. Nearer and nearer she'd hear them come. And then . . . nothing. The door stayed stubbornly closed and the handle refused to turn. And Phumla had been gone so long she could have been to the shop and back ten times, thought her mother, throwing surreptitious glances at her husband.

Trying hard not to look worried but with growing frequency, Nolungile went to peer out of the door. Soon, she had positioned herself there, and then she began calling the child's name. When that brought little result, the mother went out to the streets. All along NY 1 between NY 3a and NY 50 the mother yelled her daughter's name: "Phumla-a-a! *We-e-e!* Phu-u-mm-laa-a! Phu-mmm-laa!"

Back to the zone went Nolungile. Now, she was beside herself with fear. "*Tata kaPhumla*," thus she addressed her husband in the manner of a Xhosa wife; "Father of Phumla, I can't find this child," in a voice barely audible, fighting back tears.

Mkwayi sat still, pondering what his wife said to him. If this child was loitering, he would have to give her a hiding. She must be stopped at once from developing bad habits. Thus, thought the husband of Nolungile; thus thought Phumla's father. But before long his own thoughts too changed. Uneasiness filled him as one who's eaten badly cooked beans is filled with gas.

Both parents left the zone to go and look for their daughter. They entertained the hope that perhaps she had lost her way, got confused perhaps by the dark, the night . . .

The crowds had thinned a bit since the time their daughter had stood in those very same doorways. From shop to shop went the couple: "*Sifunisa nqentwazanana.*" They repeated their anxious mission: "We are looking for a little girl." They stopped all they met, men and women and children too. In none of the tiny one-room shops did they find Phumla. Not in the shops on NY 50, nor around the corner at those on NY 3a. None of the children still playing around the shops remembered a girl fitting the description Phumla's parents gave.

Convinced she had returned during their absence, the pair went back to the zone, sure they would find their daughter there. But Phumla had not returned. Even the other men at this zone got out of their beds or stopped whatever else they were doing, and helped in the search for the missing child: knocking on doors and yelling her name to the air — "Phuu-mmm-la-a-a!"

"She is this high," arm outstretched, palm down, strangers were asked if they had seen a little girl wearing a blue and pink flannel petticoat. None had seen Phumla.

By eleven o'clock, Mkwayi and the group of men from his own zone and from neighboring zones broke into smaller groups and ventured into the family houses across from the Single Men's Hostels. Other women from the same zones took care of Nodoli and kept the search party on its feet; with tea or coffee or bread: anything to keep them going.

About four in the morning, it was decided the search should be resumed in the morning. The father would not go to work. One of those helping, and who happened to work at the same place as Mkwayi, said he would tell the *mlungu* why he was not at work. After that, all went to their respective sleeping rooms to try and catch a wink before going to work in a few hours.

Guguletu people do not go to the police until they see that not to do so would land them in more trouble than they were in already. Phumla's parents had some idea they should go and tell the police their little girl was missing. But they still hoped they would not have to do that . . . that there was some explanation for Phumla's not returning from the shop . . . that, early in the morning, some adult would come with Phumla saying, "She was in some danger and I took her home overnight. Are you her parents?" And all would be well once more.

Throughout what remained of the night, Nolungile and her husband talked about nothing else but the disappearance of the child. And going to the police in the morning, as soon as the buses started running. In hushed whispers so as not to wake the other people in the zone, they looked at their problem from all possible angles and consoled each other although they had not acknowledged their loss.

With the roar of the bus that picks up the bus drivers from Guguletu,

Mkwayi was up. He lighted the primus stove, warmed the water he would wash in, and made some coffee. Today, he did not wait for Nolungile to do this. He knew how heavy her heart was . . . and she had not had any sleep at all. He had heard her stifled sobs and felt the wetness from her eyes.

As Mkwayi gave his wife a mug of coffee he noted that neither of the two of them had even taken off the clothes they wore the day before.

Mkwayi took his hat and, not looking at his wife's swollen eyes, avoiding her seeing his own, red, he said, "*Mhlawumbi lo mntwana uya kuba sel'elaph 'ukubuya kwam. Mandiye.* Maybe this child will be here when I return. Let me go," and he made his way to the bus stop.

At Shop Ten, the butchery, one of the young men working there went to the open yard at the back of the shop. His morning duties included burning the refuse in the drum that stood suspended between two poles to prevent the dogs that roam the township foraging for food from upsetting the trash and scattering refuse on the ground. The young man, kerosene bottle in hand, came close to the drum in order to see whether or not he needed to use the kerosene. If the drum had a lot of paper and other highly inflammable materials he would not use the kerosene.

"*Thixo Wam! Thixo Wam*! My God. My God." The young man stumbled back into the shop. His eyes were on stalks, his mouth agape, and tremors shook him.

"*Bhuti*, come and see what I found in the drum." The choked words startled the man to whom they were addressed and, like a magnet, pulled him to the drum.

He was the butcher; a short, balding man whose abdomen reminded one of a barrel or Humpty Dumpty. Unfortunately, his spindly legs did nothing to dispel the illusion. Now, he waddled out of the shop and towards the drum.

"Almighty, Lord God!" he gasped, beating a hasty retreat. "Selby!" he hollered to his son manning both register and telephone, "*Kwedini*, call the police. Call the police," he repeated. Seeing the look of stupor on his son's face, he added. "There's a child's body at the back." He couldn't bring himself to say the body was in the garbage can.

He thought: Dear God, what is the world coming to? Sweat-drenched, he felt his knees tire of the thankless job of forever holding up the rest of the body. Limply, he let himself fall onto a chair. He was cold, very cold. On a sun-washed morning, he was cold as the carcasses in the deep freeze at the back of his shop. Like wildfire, news of the body of a child, a little girl, about five or six years old, spread throughout that part of the township. It even crossed impenetrable boundaries — from the shops it flew to the homes, leapt across the invisible barrier, and into the zones. But, fortunately, it missed Nolungile.

First, two running figures made their way to the spot, then two more, then more, and then still more. Before long, a crowd formed at the scene of the terrible find.

Mkwayi, still waiting at the bus stop, saw one of the helpers in the previous night's search. "Where to, Tshawe?" he asked, "and why such haste so early in the morning?"

When the man told him he was going to see if there was any truth to the rumor of a child found hurt near the shops, Mkwayi would not hear of not accompanying his neighbor although the latter tried to dissuade him from doing so. Like condemned prisoners going to the gallows, the two crossed NY 1 and made their way to the shops.

The police van thudded to a bumpy halt just as they neared the crowd. Bang-bang, the sound of doors being slammed hushed those gathered around the drum. Eyes turned to the two white men who'd just jumped from the van even before the engine had stopped roaring.

Moses' staff had no greater magic in parting the sea. As the police approached, a natural parting appeared; the crowd dividing to give them easy passage. They didn't need to utter a single word.

A queer marriage of fear and hope made Mkwayi bold. "Let me pass. Please, let me pass. We have a daughter missing, let me pass." And as healthy people hasten to make room for a leper, the crowd fell back filled with anticipation. This man might be the father of the horrible thing in that rubbish drum. He might be so linked to the horror most had only heard whispered.

Mkwayi came up to the police who were peering into the drum and barking into the walkie talkie. He stood alone, his neighbor having fallen a little behind to differentiate the one directly affected from a mere friend.

"Back! Go back, this is police business!" One of the men in uniform yelled. And Mkwayi found that unbeknown to him, a dog had eaten his tongue. He wanted to say: "Please, sir, let me look inside that drum. I'm sure that is not my daughter, Phumla, my eldest child. But, please let me look." But the words would not allow themselves to be uttered.

Someone, a faceless woman from the crowd, shouted: "He is the child's father!" And made sure her face did not look that bold . . . like the face of someone who had dared answer the police when they had asked her nothing at all. She knew her place. The place she was stepping from. She knew her place and knew, too, if she forgot it, those two men would not hesitate to put her back in it. They were the police. And, in their eyes, she was nobody.

However, her intervention did the trick. For the briefest moment, the two men forgot *their place* and became just ordinary men, human beings: no more and no less.

They looked at the man standing there, slightly forward from the rest of the riff-raff. They looked at him and, without saying one word, not a word, just by their demeanor — being, why, just people — Mkwayi knew he could proceed, come nearer where they stood.

Seeing him thus treated, his friend approached and the two approached the ominous drum together. One look. That's all it took. One look. And the other man had no more doubt. Blindly he turned and walked away. He knew the grotesque shape was Mkwayi's daughter. He had gone several slow steps when he suddenly stopped, seemed to remember something, turned back, and walked back to the man still standing . . . still staring . . . into the wicked mouth of the rusty metal drum.

Meneer Daniel Louw, the Dominee of the church where the van Niekerk's worshipped, rang the bell and, without waiting to be admitted, opened the door and walked in. "*Môre, almal.*" His booming voice sent ripples throughout the mourning house. The Dominee was not one to tread softly. He had phoned Piet as soon as he'd finished breakfast, at half past six. He had a large flock and was a busy man. A direct man.

Piet, the Dominee, and the two grandfathers sat around the dining-room table. Hilda had put on it a large coffee pot and a heaped platter of *koesisters*. Now, the men went over business. The older men seemed to have recovered somewhat following the night's sleep. Piet was red-eyed, his face gaunt as one who hadn't slept for weeks. And each word had to be dragged out of him. He was vague and absent-minded; like someone suffering from jet lag. But, by and by the man of God stood up and took his leave. No one could make the little group he was leaving cheerful. That was not what he had come to do. But, he did leave them a little more at peace, having made plans for them to lay their beloved little one to rest.

Tshawe laid a hand on his friend's shoulder. He had no words to say and just wanted the other to know he was there, with him. He had decided he'd follow Mkwayi's lead.

Mkwayi was like a man awakened from deep sleep. He turned and looked at his friend as at one he had never seen before. Slowly, his head turned this way and that way as if he was trying to find a face among the crowd, a face he knew or remembered, a face that restored meaning to whatever was going on in his mind, a face that filled the void, the lacunae deep within, the thing that threatened to rob him of all breath.

All at once, understanding shone through his eyes. He had come back from wherever it was he had gone to. Now he knew exactly where he was and why he was where he was.

Mkwayi roared like a wounded bull. He reached into the drum and, before the police realized what was happening, had the bizarre shape halfway out.

One of the policemen sprung to action as some people screamed. In a wink, he'd snatched the body from Mkwayi. Someone came forward with a blanket and the body was laid on the ground and covered. The older policeman led Mkwayi firmly but gently away. The three men, Mkwayi and policeman, with Tshawe trailing them, wearily trod their way to the van standing less than three yards away.

"Wait here. You have to come to the police station with us." And Tshawe joined his friend at the back of the police van; the door wide open, neither had even an inkling of escaping. Their heavy hearts locked the wide open door more securely than the heaviest and strongest lock. There they sat. And waited. Mkwayi's eyes were water-logged, but he didn't know this, and had he known, he wouldn't have cared. As tears washed his cheeks, Mkwayi saw the mother of his child . . . his child folded and misshapen; deformed. Clearly, he saw Nolungile, saw her as if she stood right there in front of his two eyes. Nolungile. What would he say to her?

Nolungile, forced out of lethargic stupor by Nodoli's cries, quickly made her a bowl of mealie meal porridge. Phumla's father, she thought, must be finished at the police station. She did not want to think any further than that. There was only one place more fearful to her than the police station: the morgue. But she also knew that her husband would not go to that place alone. He would come back and ask someone to accompany him there if . . .

There, Nolungile's thoughts refused to go on.

Meanwhile, the morning paper, the *Cape Times*, carried the story of the child murdered on the beach. Front page, the story made. Complete with a picture of where the body was found. In the picture, a big black X marked where Nina had lain. Of course, those with radios and TV heard (or saw) the story the night before. It had made the seven o'clock bulletin, albeit in sketchy detail. Fuller coverage came at eleven. And in the manner of the media, viewers were told the parents were too distraught to answer questions. Which meant someone had actually gone to these parents of a dead child, a child killed in blood, slain by a maniac . . . but the interviewer(s) had gone to such parents and asked them questions.

What kind of questions does one ask people whom such horror has visited: "Excuse me, but are you grieving?" No, maybe it is more something like, "When last did you see your child?" Or, "Will you miss her?"

Why are such questions necessary? And why at such a time? Cannot they wait?

Around the shops and away from the center of attraction, the day had woken. Children with milk bottles hurried home where, no doubt, morning coffees were on the brew. The bus stop had its normal Saturday morning crowd — workers and shoppers. But, to all this Mkwayi was blind. His world lay at his feet, a long, hard, thorn-filled road to his wife.

Nolungile was feeding the child when Mkwayi walked in through the door and, without a single word, let her know her first-born child was gone. Was no more.

The enamel bowl flew away from her hand and clattered onto the cement floor. Someone grabbed Nodoli as Nolungile slid from the wooden bench. She heard the keening from high above her and far away, a long distance away. Two of the women who had walked in with Mkwayi rushed to her aid while the men packed up the meager furnishings, preparing the room for a wake.

Two little girls were dead. The families devastated.

"CLEAN UP SEA POINT" screamed the headlines for weeks after. And the dirt, the scum alluded to, was other human beings whose otherness set them apart, rendered them so unlike the owners of the strident voices all raised in holy ire.

For a period thereafter, pass arrests soared, vagrancy was curbed with ruthless zeal. Any black person seen "abroad" after a certain hour had to answer testing questions posed in the rudest manner. A curfew had come to Cape Town. What would the city have done had it known of Nina's death twin? Of six-year-old Phumla Dyantyi whom a full-grown man had ravaged as a whore? And then strangled her and stuffed her lifeless body into a trash can. In crouch position?

What would the city have done had it seen how, to fit the little corpse into a coffin, the knees had to be sawed because rigor mortis had set in in crouch position?

Today, no one knows the name of the little girl found in a rubbish drum at the back of the butcher's shop. They don't know it today, for they never knew it then.

Even the few who remember the sad tale often wonder what her name was. Since the story never made the news, most never knew her name. They only remember how her knees had to be sawed to fit her into a coffin.

And yet, not a few remember the name Nina van Niekerk. In

Guguletu. After all these years . . . more than ten.

They remember the sorrow. The grief of mothers. The murder of innocent little girls. In Cape Town. They remember the horror. And, to this day they still wonder, how they found themselves foremost among suspects. Great sorrow. And burning anger.

17

Now that the pass has gone

Perhaps it is because I have experienced a pass arrest only three times in my life; and on none of these three occasions did I spend a night in the police cells. The first took place one evening on my way from work. I had just stepped off the bus and was about to start the five-minute walk to my home. Luckily for me, someone who witnessed the arrest ran to my house and told my children. This same person then picked up the pass I had inadvertently left behind that morning, brought it to the police station and waited there because the van was still on patrol. When, six hours later, the van returned to base, I was released. I had been greatly inconvenienced, scared out of my mind, humiliated beyond belief — yes; but I had not been locked overnight in a police cell with hardened criminals. For that, I was grateful.

The second and third times, I had to pay an admission of guilt fine. A distinct hardship given the low wages I earned, my five children, and the fact that I am a single parent. But Mother borrowed this from that person and that from this person and, on both occasions, raised the fifty rands fine and came and got me. Neighbors and friends pitched in to raise the fine; that being the only insurance they carry against the time adversity comes a-knocking at their own doors.

All in all therefore, I consider myself very fortunate in the matter of the pass. One hears such horrendous stories of people who have been molested, raped, and otherwise violated . . . because of the pass. I know these terrible things have happened, and in view of that, what has happened to me, as far as the pass is concerned, is tolerable.

Perhaps I was just plain glad those horrible things would never happen to me. Or, perhaps I was relieved at the opportunity to put the whole sad pass page of our history to rest, to run away from unpleasant memories, from a past too pain-filled, too raw to store. I don't know. Human nature is frail. I am only too human. But now, looking back, I admit there may have been an element of cowardly glee, exhilaration if you like, at the knowledge I had not been put through the worst . . . by the pass; and now, with the pass gone, a thing of the past, I need not fear that eventuality. I was free. At least, from this one menace.

The euphoria, of course, was not of my manufacturing or the result of my imagination. In 1987, the unthinkable had happened. The pass laws were rescinded. The pass was no more. It was dead. The jubilation! Never had I seen Africans so united in joy; except perhaps the day Doctor Verwoerd was assassinated.

Throughout that dizzy month of April, the media — radio, print, television — S-C-R-E-A-M-E-D: THE PASS HAS GONE!

Even that stalwart of Afrikaner Nationalism, the NGK, voiced cautious support, praising the Government's "ushering in a new era in the history of the country."

Hopes were high. Black people were ecstatic. With the pass gone, they reasoned, could *uhuru* be far behind? And abroad, from black and from white. We all wore glee like a banner; relieved from the scourge of the pass.

My annoyance at my mother is thus understandable. When people in the African townships, in squatter camps, in villages, in resettlement areas, and in "other" classified residential areas where they remained thus breaking the law, when all these people joined and, as one, heaved a gigantic common sigh of relief and praise . . . who would dare be the exceptions? Who could complain? . . . raining on our national celebrations?

Like a sore tooth that will stick out longer than every other in one's mouth — Mother wore the face of a widow who, upon waking up one *shushu* morning, discovers the family's only daughter, for whom *lobola* has been fully paid, has eloped with the local ne'er-do-well who thus abandons a pregnant wife, six children, and a frail, aged and toothless mother. Can such a widow, such a mother of such a daughter, give the other daughter instead of the silly disgraceful one who had eloped? Can she repay the *lobola* — some of which she had pledged as payment for the wedding? Can her dead husband go to the mines, work out a stint or two, and repay the *lobola*?

"White people know how to play with us. Really, we are toys to them. Truly, truly I am old. That I have lived to see a day such as this.

"Today they say the pass has gone. Where did it go? Who sent it wherever it is that it has gone? Where had it ever come from, and why? Why was it ever here? And why only for us? And who says it can never come back? Had we known once that we would live, have to live, with it?

"*Yhuu!* My child, long have I lived. This is a day that swallows all other days. I tell you, this is some day this."

Thus my mother lamented what we all celebrated. Her irrationality surpassed all understanding. "A saint would've throttled her," I thought.

That night, thinking to redeem my fast-evaporating filial feelings: "Mother," I said, "what is it that is bothering you about this?"

It was two nights later and I had almost forgotten my irritation when, out of her uncharacteristic moodiness, Mother asked, "Do you remember the time *Bhuti* was so ill we all thought he really was dying?"

"Mmh mhm?" I had no idea where this was leading to and my attention was focused on our new Sony TV and that is where I wanted my eyes and my mind to dwell right now. But my mother takes hints at her own convenience. She had something to say and would say it, with or without my help.

"Do you remember the story of China, the young man whose wife greeted his return with hands on her head and threw her voice to the four corners of the earth wailing as if she had just been told her favorite twins had drowned?"

That sure got her the attention she wanted; my concentration broke as my mind zoomed back to a time, some ten or so years gone.

Mother's eldest brother, retired and living not far from the village where he was born, in the Transkei, had taken gravely ill.

We, all three of us, Mother's surviving children, put some money together and got her a train ticket and off she went to be by his bedside.

A month or two later Mother had returned. Her brother was mending. The scare was over. It was while she was recounting her journey that she had told us of this story one evening.

Her face had arranged itself as if the day were a Saturday and it was the afternoon and its owner was going to a funeral:

"The pass has killed the people. Yes, it has killed off a lot of people.

"We had a long wait at Umtata station. There was a delay. Some people resorted to buses, but even those couldn't take many. They arrived there almost full already. And no bus, no matter how big it is or how many in number, can take the people a train can carry. Well, as we sat their waiting I noticed a man, a very young man . . . the age recently married or soon to be married or busy looking for a wife. Yes, he was no boy but he was still green in manhood.

"I don't quite know how it started, but before long we were sending him to the café for coffee, sweets, Extra Strong, or Disprins. I first noticed him retrieving cool-drink cans and bottles from the garbage. Then quietly, he approached us saying, '*BooMama* (Mothers), please do not throw away any food you can't finish. I'm hungry.' My child . . . for a man-child to plead for food, to beg for others' *slaps* . . . what others cast away when they have had enough . . . something gnawed at the deep of my stomach, deep where the memory of my own motherhood lies awake.

"I gave him some bread and a piece of my chicken. '*Enkosi, Mama.*' He accepted the food, sat down, and very, very slowly, ate it. I tell you, he chewed on each morsel as though he wanted his teeth, his tongue, the saliva in his mouth, the very walls of his mouth to remember . . . and not bother him soon about their need for a repeat performance.

"When he had finished, I asked him to get us something to drink —

coffee for me and tea, coffee or a cool drink for himself.

"Thanking me, he declined the drink saying, 'If you don't mind, I would rather keep the money for I have nothing . . . not a cent on me.'

'Of course,' I said, 'you can keep the money.' When he returned with my coffee I gave him two rands. Do you know that when he saw what I gave him, tears started down his face?

"Oh, *Mntan'am*, don't talk to me about the pass. That serpent has killed our people."

The young man, said Mother, told her and those in that waiting room this tale: He said, "Mama, life is hard. Life, indeed, is very hard."

His name was China, he said, and he was of the Majola clan. He had three stints in the mines of Jo'burg under his belt. At the end of his last contract he had returned planning a longer than usual stay in the village, for he was to take a wife. That was six months before his meeting Mother. In his own words:

"I was with my *makoti*, my new wife, Nomonde (Mother of Patience), only six weeks before I left her to come here to get a *join* from the village. The chiefs and the headmen scratch only for their own families. But then, *amaXhosa* do say, 'No pheasant scratches the ground for another;' any that does has chicks.

"Word was Umtata was the best town if one wanted a *join*. The recruiter preferred it because, being a bigger town, it has hotels, bars, and other places of interest to gentlemen far from their own families. So to Umtata I came.

"My poor little wife. She plucked a chicken for me. She kneaded bread, and made my provisions: the chicken was brown like the chicken one buys from the Take Away shops. And, she'd cooked it whole.

"I asked her who had taught her to cook like that and she answered, shyly, 'Makhulu. She used to work for white people.' I said when I returned from my *join* I would voluntarily go to her father and give him more *lobola*. We both laughed at this and she could see I was very happy with her.

"My wife. A real marvel. Young. Beautiful. And very shy. And yet she is so accomplished around the house. I knew I'd done well taking for a wife the young woman my mother pointed to me saying, 'China, there is a wife, a young woman who will build a home for the young man bright enough to snatch her before wolves get her.'"

He was smiling, remembering his young wife and her ways. Several people in that waiting-room chuckled, amused at the earnestness of young love. An elderly man who had seemed asleep throughout suddenly spoke startling us all: "*He, Mfo wam*, hey, my young man," he said in a deep, low voice — like the rumblings of faraway thunder, "come and tell us how good your wife is when your eldest child can be sent to the river to draw water, then we'll listen. Now, all we hear is the melodious song of warm blankets. Let me tell you, that song is as old as these mountains you see pimpling the land." Everyone laughed at this and not a few agreed that all new love, indeed, did entrance. But there were those who averred that love, properly nourished, could continue to enthrall to the sweet end. These voices, few and mostly female, must have encouraged the young man for he continued:

"Will you believe me when I say she baked the bread using only an old ragged sack? That is the truth . . . the pure and simple truth . . . mmhmmh mmhh.

"Yes, I saw her with my own two eyes — take a sack and roll the *bakpot* in it. After she'd secured the sack firmly, making sure it layered the iron pot evenly, she set a light to the sack. Would you believe that after that sack was burnt to nothing but ash the bread was done? And softer, moister bread you've never seen. It melted like sugar in my mouth. In the wicker basket she also put some eggs and salt, two bottles of ginger beer — this too, she'd made herself. She sent me off like that . . . like a man who has a loving wife who knows he leaves her only to go and work for her. It was a Sunday when I left. The third Sunday of the month of Pleiades; June. My hopes were high. Soon, I thought, I would get parcels of nice things I would buy for her. I had noticed her stingy father had sent her to me with only one pair of shoes — although I had given him so much *lobola*. But, I didn't mind. As long as I had my strength, I vowed, she would want for nothing."

He left home in that time of night when all but the very sick are dead to the world. He wanted to be in Umtata before the sun, and, indeed, bright and early on Monday morning, he reached the town.

"What I found here was frightening. People, men of all age-groups . . . they were waiting . . . they were all waiting to get *joins*.

"You see, for five years now the fields have given us nothing. Rain is gone from these parts. We hear of torrents in cities such as P.E. and East London . . . even up north, we hear of houses submerged under water . . . *amajoyini* from these far away places return with such stories of heavy rains stopping cars and buses . . . even trains, uprooting trees, and demolishing houses or turning them upside down. But here, where our lives depend on rain . . . we do not see any rains.

"The shops had not opened when the first trucks came, and we were like herds of cattle from different villages being dipped in the same dip trench. The bosses, the boers who come sitting next to the men driving these trucks, the men who would interpret for the bosses — because most of them can't speak our language — they were men who looked well fed and in good health. They were red from the heat in their trucks and wore short trousers, short-sleeved shirts although it was winter.

"Each truck would pull up and the black man, the driver, would jump out hollering — Funarhen! or Jemistin! or Cape Town! or Durban! that told us where his truck came from . . . where the *join* was from.

"As each new truck roared into sight bunches of men would shove into position . . . all around the truck. Everyone wanted to be up front near the boss, for it is he who points out the men he chooses. The boss picks. So it is his eye that you pray will fall on you and will like you.

"These bosses don't ask anyone anything. Only their eyes choose. They are not interested in how hard you work, where you have worked before or nothing. They just look and pick.

"No, Mothers, they look for strong men. They look at how tall you are, whether you have muscle or you're just skin and bones. They want to pick men who look like they had food to eat the last two weeks. They don't want a man who has been starving. Such a man's health may be breaking. The bosses don't want a bull that's on its last legs . . . no, they do not want such a one.

"That day only, ten trucks came looking for boys. But I was not one of the lucky ones; I was not picked. If I had not seen some of the men I'd found here wipe away tears as the last of the trucks roared away leaving them behind, I would not have been that worried. But these men's tears made my knees like those of a baby who's fallen as he took his first tentative steps.

"That evening, I ate for the first time since I had left home. I did not want to chase my provisions away. What would I eat then if I let the food disappear fast? I had no money on me . . . only four rands. Four rands and thirty-two cents. That's all."

"*Mntan'am*, that poor boy ended up chasing his food anyway. Chicken will only last three to four days, you know? Even in winter it will not stay unspoilt for a whole week. So, by the end of the week, his food was gone . . . but he was still in Umtata. He told us that the shorter men were at a distinct disadvantage. And he himself was no tall man. The bosses wanted tall, well-built, well-fed men.

"It was a competition among all of us," he said.

"Day in and day out, we tried to look better and healthier and stronger than all the men near us. Five hundred men. Every day, there, competing with each other. Every day, about a hundred were picked and they left praising their ancestors who had delivered them from this miserable human auction. It was rumored that to help their luck along, some of the men went and paid the drivers who came with the recruiters, so that they could put in a good word for them. Others sought the services of witchdoctors and medicine men. Of course, everybody prayed to the Almighty. And as fast as the lucky ones left, others flocked in from the villages: an unending stream of despairing hope; more swarmed in than the numbers leaving, going away on contract to some faraway city or farm. And the human residue, the rejects, forever swelled by the numbers of fresh arrivals who thought they knew what they were in for, husbanded their meager strength for the competition next time around; hopeful still that that would be their lucky day. That is what the pass did to us. It fenced us in. We could only graze here and not over there. And here, where we were fenced in, where our best chance was, there was nothing. A big fat nothing. Only starvation.

"Although most men were hungry most of the time, most, after two weeks in Umtata, had neither food nor money left. I know after two weeks my stomach and my pocket were as flat as bugs in a deserted house.

"However, as soon as a truck appeared, by the time the boss got out or sat there looking out of the window of his truck or stood at the back of his truck — you know, to give himself vantage point — do you know what? Every man was out there trying to outdo all the rest put together in looking his most robust self. Each man pulled his neck to the heavens, puffed out his chest like a cock courting a hen, opened his eyes wide alert to show the boss he's an intelligent, honest boy, and pulled his lips sideways until they imperiled his ears. Every man wanted to be seen as friendly and not a cheeky boy. I heard say some men even stood on their toes, all the time. One man fell and broke a tooth . . . because while he was grinning up to the boss one of the two empty cans of jam he stood on gave way, sending him toppling over.

"By week three I became alarmed. My position was serious. No food. No money. And my hope dimmed for the first time here. Every day, I had hoped . . . every day, in my heart, a big, fat hope sat there smiling. I just knew one of the bosses would see — couldn't help but see, what a good boy I am. I am, you know. And I just knew that truth would shine out and I would soon be picked for a *join*.

"A few of us made friends with workers here in the town and they helped us here and there. But these are people whose own situations are not that secure that they can spend time helping anyone. Some take a big risk just letting one person come and visit them where they work. If their boss finds you washing in his boy's or girl's room . . . that person will be in trouble, big trouble. So, it was the river for most of us . . . for most of the time . . . for washing. And the forest for other things.

"I did not know what I would say to my mother and my wife. I knew we had nothing back home; I had left them with nothing but the hope that I was leaving to go and find work and send them money so they could live. And now I was returning. What would I say to them? I knew that they looked out for people returning from the shop, each day, so they could hear if there was a letter there for them. They knew I'd send them money as soon as I got my first pay. And since I'd been away for more than a month, why wouldn't they have begun expecting money? It was not an unreasonable expectation. How could they know I was still here in Umtata? How could they know no boss saw me as a good boy? No, they waited, thinking

I was far away; thinking I was working and they would soon receive money from me.

"The long walk home was torture. With each step I asked myself: What will you say to them? What will you say? The answer did not come to me and I was still asking myself this question when, there I was, looking down from the hill . . . at my home . . . looking at it and frightened like a child facing a wild animal whose name he does not know. What would they say?, I wondered. How would I be received?"

Shaking his shoulders, he had picked up the bundle at his feet. Down he went, slowly . . . treading as if each foot had to think about what it was doing. Now, he was shouting-distance away. He made no sound; creeping towards his home like a thief or a wizard come by night. He came to the back of the *rondavels.* He could hear voices from within, but the sound of his galloping heart was louder than all those voices put together. Again he stood stock still and thought: I can go left to the hut I share with my *makoti* or I can go right and meet everyone at the same time.

A door creaked open. "*Voetsek! Phandle!*" That was Vusi's voice. Vusumzi, his younger brother, was shooing the dog out. Yelp, yelp, yelp; and the dog stopped short, no doubt sniffing his scent. It growled, taking the decision out of his hands. Whistling low, he snapped his fingers: creak creak creak; and dog's ears flew up and its growl changed to a puzzled whine and then a series of joy-filled grunts; its tail wagging furiously.

"Verwoerd?" Vusi shouted as he opened the door again. He peered around the hut and saw his *bhuti.*

"*UBhuti! Nank'uBhuti*! Older Brother. Here is Older Brother." And taking the empty provision basket from him, Vusi preceded his older brother into the hut; the dog, Verwoerd, all over between their legs, tail a-wagging and red tongue lashing in and out, in and out of his shiny wet mouth.

"I shook hands with Mother and with Nomonde. And both tried to hide their eyes from mine. It was easier for Nomonde to do this. Being a *makoti*, the black *doek* she wore was low over her eyes."

Nomande's eyes were down. She did not want her husband to see her fear and her disappointment and her shame. She was glad her new-wife headgear hid her eyes. Her heart had stopped when he walked in through the door. No *join* could be that short. His being here could only mean one thing. He was ill and the bosses had sent him back. How long did he work? One month? Less? Her breath came in short gulps. The air had thickened, becoming heavy. Taking a simple breath was laborious, cumbersome, and painful. What were they to do?

"I had not seen Mother cry since Father left us. Vusi was a baby then and now he is in Standard Five. But now she was crying. Oh, she tried to hide her tears: 'The smoke is burning my eyes. This wood is wet. Wet wood always burns badly and fills the house with smoke.' I knew it killed her to see me walk back into the house I'd left seven weeks before, walk back empty handed. But what pierced her heart was to see my young wife cry . . . Mother was not fooled. She knew Nomonde was crying, in her heart. And with her eyes."

Later that same night, in their little *entangeni*, the hut set aside for the young, Nomonde asked; "*Xa ubuya uthi masiihini*?" (Seeing that you return, what do you propose we do?) Quietly, the words spilled out of her young mouth; and surprised them both. Thus laden with hopelessness they were. They were a strange welcome from a bride of less than three months to her brand new husband. Very strange words. Naked in their acerbity.

Stranger still was that the husband had no words to answer them. Although he had rehearsed, for the past twelve hours, what he would say to his wife, when he came face to face with her, he lost all knowledge of what to say . . . how to explain his return.

"Before the week was over, I was certain of only one thing. I had made a big mistake going back. We lived through others' kindness. That wife of mine was like a starving sow with a large litter. A web of footpaths sprung between our huts and neighboring homesteads. Every morning and every evening she had to go to that one for milk, go to the other one for sugar. Should she get flour from the woman she still owes beans? And yeast? Now that she had the flour, whom should she see for the yeast? The neighbors behind us were seen carrying half a bag of mealie-meal from the shop, surely, they could spare us just one, one basinful? Rumor had it that Maxolo's husband had sent her some money from the mines in Kimberley. Nomonde was at her house before cock crow next morning: the whole village was hungry. She had to make sure others didn't beat her to it. We were not the only people with ears to hear.

"Yes, I saw, we could not live like that. If I stayed, I would be a dead man. No, worse, *isithunzela*, a zombie. A dead man needs no food. I needed food. I ate when Mother and Nomonde ate. I even stooped to eating *umfino*. And for a man to eat food that even a boy wouldn't be seen eating . . . that is when I knew I could not stay."

Two days later, the young man was back in Umtata. He had been gone less than ten days. Mother said that when she came upon him in the tiny South African Railways waiting-room in Umtata, he had been back there for more than three months. The second leaving had had little preparation, no provisions; and the tears that bade him farewell then were not about the pain of separation, of love denied. Those tears sprang from naked fear.

Sometimes he came to watch the recruiters' trucks. To watch the human auction that had stamped him REJECT. Now, he was an onlooker, outside of it all. He collected discarded beer- and cool-drink cans and bottles. It was the money that he got from these that he took back to his mother and his wife. He saw them once a month. They had no idea what kind of work he was doing. But that was all he could give them; and he gave that all to them. For himself? Well, the people in the waiting-room . . . some of them, were very kind. If he went to the shop for them, helped them with their luggage, little things like that, well . . . some gave him money, others gave him food; a little goes a long way . . . a very long way. The money he got from his "job," that he must take home. His mother had Vusi to feed and send to school and . . . well, his wife told him there might be new eyes to look into his come Easter. Nopasika, if it was a girl. He liked that name. Nopasika: She who comes at Pasch.

So Mother turned my mind to stories such as this story of Nomonde's husband, China; stories about the hardship, the hurts and the humiliation the pass has inflicted on the African people.

I wonder if China ever got the contract he so desperately needed. Where is he now? Did they survive the ravages of dire need, grueling need, dirt-poor existence? Did they make it to these days of NOW, THE PASS HAS GONE? And, if so, what scars will always be theirs . . . the inheritancc of a willed deprivation, of allocated penury, a pass-controlled poverty?

I started out fighting Mother because she felt no joy that the pass has gone. And here I am, not only agreeing with her. At least she was calm about her misgivings. I, who had thought her unreasonable, I am fit to be tied. For I have not escaped the ravages of the pass. None of us has escaped. The pass is in our very souls.

And *I* berated her? She is so wise, this mother of mine. Now I know the pain, the sorrow of her vision, watching us dancing on our grave. Now I see what she tried to tell me: The pass has gone; the pass will never die.

Yet, the millions of Chinas: children, men, women — in their millions, bonsaid . . . by the pass — have they not survived? Just by being alive, being here to tell the tale, have they not triumphed? Now that the pass has gone, deep down will the roots go; and the tree shall burst the sweetest of fruit amidst blazing flower. Surely, now that the pass has gone . . . surely, the starved and shriveled roots will swell and spread and throb, shooting branches far and wide. Surely, the time is now, now that the pass has gone.